Bones Takes a Holiday

Dr. Benjamin Bones Mysteries
Book 3

Emma Jameson

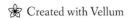

For all of Dr. Bones and Lady Juliet's fans, with love

Dr. Bones and the Christmas Wish

Chapter One

D r. Benjamin Bones had no opinion on Christmas. That is to say, he had no *polite* opinion on Christmas. His actual opinion, the one he knew better than to say aloud, was that Christmas was a disappointment, a raising of hopes only to dash them, a festival of flash and dazzle which, come January, was hard to pay for and even harder to justify. That was Christmas: disappointment, with a price tag.

It didn't help that Cornwall, famously temperate compared to the rest of England, had turned bitterly cold. Or that the cold made his recently injured left leg ache in the morning and throb all night. Or that the woman who'd been right in front of him, the woman he'd found himself falling in love with, could never be his.

She's back with her husband. I should be happy for her, he told himself.

His reflection scowled at him from the window of a secondhand shop. His coat collar was turned up, his red scarf double-wrapped, his fedora pulled low. In Ben's native London, these clues, along with the grim set of his mouth, would have signaled passersby to give him a wide berth. In his adopted village of Birdswing, they had no effect whatsoever on the residents, who ranged from sociable to pathologically friendly.

"Oh! Dr. Bones. I hate to interrupt," said Mrs. Parry. Her booming voice would have told him who was speaking, even if he couldn't see the heavy, buxom woman in the gray coat cruising up slowly, like a battleship, behind him. "But you've been standing outside Howell's for five minutes. Are you quite all right?"

He took a deep breath. Mrs. Parry sounded sweetly concerned, but then she always did. She lived directly across the street from him, and whenever he so much as stepped out to take the air, her white lace curtains twitched. If Special Constable Gaston knocked on his door, or Lady Juliet roared up in her Crossley, Mrs. Parry invented some reason to wander over for a closer look. She knew his affairs as well as he did, perhaps better. For a moment Ben was tempted to say so.

But looking into her face, he just couldn't. Mrs. Parry was a Nosy Parker of the first degree, but that didn't make her concern for him any less genuine. Her gaze was soft; the corners of her mouth turned up hopefully. Her son had been killed in the Great War; both her daughters had married and gone away. A young widower like Ben triggered both her instinct to snoop and her desire to nurture.

"Has it been five minutes? I didn't notice. Hallo, Mrs. Parry." Ben lifted his hat the way his father had taught him ("All the way up, son. Show daylight between your hat and your hair, none of this brim-touching nonsense.") and smiled. "What sort of errand are you on? Christmas shopping?"

"Good heavens, no. I go to market in the morning, like a civilized woman," she said, looking over her shoulder at the sun, which would set in less than an hour. "I dashed out in search of a mermaid."

"Beg pardon?"

"A mermaid," Mrs. Parry repeated. "A very particular one, for my friend Mrs. Smith. I'm afraid if I don't find it, and bring it to her soon...." She glanced both ways to be sure she wasn't overheard before finishing softly, "She'll die."

4

"Letty Smith?" It was too cold to linger outside Howell's Nonesuch, a grandiose name for a modest little shop with frying pans and calico aprons in the front window. "Come inside and tell me. When I looked in on her last month, she seemed comfortable enough."

The bell tinkled overhead as Ben opened the door for Mrs. Parry. She entered at an angle, as the shops along this stretch of Birdswing's high street had been built around 1845, when materials were scarcer, Cornishmen were smaller, or the knackers—those tiny mischief-makers said to live in old mineshafts—drafted the plans according to their personal needs. A heroically-built woman like Mrs. Parry had to squeeze through the doorway, while Ben, though only five foot eight, had to duck his head in order to enter.

Stepping into Howell's Nonesuch was like stepping into the pages of a children's fairy tale—one with shoddy line drawings and only a rare splash of color. The low ceiling appeared even lower because of the detritus hung from the rafters: a scooter, roller skates, a sled, and one of those iron "beaters" used to knock the dust (and dust mites) out of bedlinens. Arranged on tables were other items, many dented or scratched: bedpan, bookends, razor strop, hernia truss, and a tea service with only three cups. Men's and women's secondhand clothes were jammed on the same bar, the hangers so tight, they would have been impossible to browse. At the back of the shop, on a stool behind the counter, sat a bald little man in a velvet coat.

If this is a fairy story, he's the shoemaker in need of some elves, Ben thought.

The little man looked up from his book. He was balding, with a few thin gray wisps on top. His face was impossibly craggy, the lines stacking up on his cheeks and nearly obscuring his eyes when he smiled. But the smile was so bright, and so broad, and so utterly real, Ben instantly revised his idea of the man.

If there's any magic here, it's in him.

"Welcome, welcome." The little man sprang up happily. He looked somewhere between seventy and two hundred, if one counted those lines like the rings inside a tree, but had the vitality of a boy.

His green eyes sparkled. "Dr. Bones, what a pleasure! And Mrs. Parry, don't you look lovely."

She made a surprised noise. "My. Yes. Thank you. Have we, er, had the pleasure? And where is Mr. Howell?"

"So sorry!" Lifting the hinged wooden countertop, the little man stepped out to greet them. "Mr. Howell is away for Christmas. He spoke so glowingly of you all, his friends in Birdswing, that I recognized you from his descriptions. Mrs. Edwina Parry, *née* Hammond, of the Penfleck Hammonds. A fine robust woman and the most attentive of neighbors."

He reached for her hand. Giggling a little, Mrs. Parry gave it, and was rewarded with a brush of lips against her knuckles.

"Oh! Charmed," she said, sounding delighted.

"And Dr. Benjamin Bones, sent to Cornwall by our government to look after the good people of Birdswing and Barking. And Plymouth, in two years. A handsome young devil outnumbered by the ladies, even in his own house."

"How do you do," Ben replied correctly, shaking the shopkeeper's hand.

"Oh, I do very well, very well indeed," the little man laughed. His velvet coat, a deep jewel green, was the most singular thing Ben had ever seen a man wear, apart from the London stage. His own wardrobe consisted of black, white, some more black, and some more white, with a couple of blue neckties for variety. He'd been brought up to believe a well turned-out man's attire drew no special attention to itself. Besides, when a physician was his age, twenty-seven, a sober wardrobe reassured his older patients that he really did know what he was doing.

"And your name is...?" Ben prompted.

"Mr. Ainsel, at your service." Grasping his emerald-green lapels, the shopkeeper drew himself to his full height of less than five feet.

"What did you mean by 'Plymouth, in two years'?" Ben asked. The villages of Birdswing, population 1,122 souls, and Barking, at around 500, kept him busy enough, even with so many men between twenty and forty already called up to service. Ben wasn't due to be seconded to Plymouth unless the city was invaded or bombed.

"Sorry! Plymouth, *I hear*," Mr. Ainsel corrected, flashing his winning smile. Unusually, for a man of his years, he had a complete set of teeth—yellow and uneven, but intact. "Now, my lovelies, what brings you into my lair? Christmas presents? I see that look! But no, no, none of that rubbish in the rafters will do. A rag and bone man would take one look and push on past. No, no, I have a trunk full of special items. Just arrived this afternoon. Only the best, I promise. Give me two minutes and I'll be back to astonish you." Without waiting for Ben and Mrs. Parry to agree, he scampered through the flimsy curtains and into the backroom.

"I couldn't say no," Mrs. Parry whispered to Ben. "All he needs is bells on his shoes, and I'd swear he works for Father Christmas."

It was very warm in the shop, so Ben loosened his scarf and unbuttoned his coat. Only when his cane clattered to the floor did he realize he'd put it aside at some point during Mr. Ainsel's introduction. His left knee, which had mended imperfectly after a serious injury, was better, too, probably because of the pervasive heat.

"Now what were you saying about Mrs. Smith? And a mermaid?"

Mrs. Parry sighed. "Letty's been my friend since we were girls. We used to swim together in Little Creek and climb the big tree in Pate's Field. Life was harder then, much harder, and all my good memories of my childhood revolve around Letty. It's hard to watch her decline and to know—" Her voice broke and she stopped, shaking her head.

"She might live another five or ten years," Ben said firmly. "I told her the same thing myself, last time I visited. Rheumatoid arthritis is a beastly disease, one of the very worst," he added, giving Mrs. Parry time to dab her eyes with a handkerchief and compose herself. "But Mrs. Smith is as strong and as brave as any patient I've seen."

"Oh, aye, she's brave," Mrs. Parry agreed. "When I was fourteen, I went to Plymouth to be a maid in a minister's townhouse. It was back-breaking work, and the wages were very low, but I did it, because it was what girls of my station did. When I couldn't bear it any longer, I set my cap at a decent man and married him. Came back to Birdswing and was a new mother at seventeen. I can't say I wanted any of it, really. But I did it, because that's what girls of my station did.

"Letty was different. She didn't like many children. She liked old people. She'd sit with them, shelling beans or knitting socks, and listen to their stories. Then she'd retell them, mix them with folktales, turn them into something meaningful. I was so proud of her," Mrs. Parry said with a smile. "Around the same time I went off to scrub doorsteps and beat rugs, she was sent to a factory to work in the laundry. But she ran away and became a bard."

"A what?"

"A bard," Mrs. Parry repeated. "She traveled up and down the West Country, all around Cornwall and through Devon, bringing songs and stories to the towns and villages. This was before the wireless, of course, when a storyteller was welcome, especially in pubs. Letty visited me once a year to tell me about her adventures. Sometimes men got the wrong idea, and she had to set them straight, but in those days, folks remembered the value of a tale well told. They bought her pints, and paid for her rooms, and bade her come back when she took her leave. It must have been glorious." Mrs. Parry sighed.

"She told me she married a farmer," Ben said.

"A gypsy, more like. She was closemouthed about him, on the main. I wish I could have seen him. I'll bet he had smoldering eyes and wild black curls."

"A gypsy named Smith?"

Mrs. Parry shrugged. "I wasn't there. When she returned to Birdswing, she came alone, except for a dark-eyed baby boy on her hip, and called herself Mrs. Smith. That was good enough for me."

Ben nodded. During his short time as Birdswing's physician, he'd already been privy to the birth of one out-of-wedlock baby. A woman with a child and no husband had few options; relocating and passing herself off as a widow was arguably the most difficult. He'd known Letty Smith was tough—anyone who contended with the agonies of rheumatoid arthritis on a daily basis was tough—but Mrs. Parry's revelation increased his respect for his patient.

"Why the mermaid?" he asked.

"Oh. When she was a bard, she loved telling the story of the Mermaid of Zennor. Have you heard it?"

He shook his head. Mrs. Parry seemed about to launch into it when Mr. Ainsel returned from the back room, curtains fluttering in his wake.

"Here 'tis, here 'tis," he cried, staggering under the weight of a brown leather trunk nearly as big as his torso. "Curios and trinkets and talismans from the four corners of the known world. Perhaps even beyond," he added with a wink, placing the trunk at Ben's feet. "Go on, Doctor. Open sesame."

Ben tried to kneel, but his left knee wasn't having it. Despite the shop's delicious warmth, it started aching again.

"Never mind," Mr. Ainsel said cheerfully, throwing open the chest himself. "If you spy something you're keen on, sing out."

Ben was startled by the sheer number of items haphazardly jumbled inside the chest. Coins, fountain pens, balls, cups, beads, pearls, bottles, cut gems so large they could only be counterfeit, dolls, rings, thimbles, and on top, a golden bracelet decorated with delicate filigreed roses.

"I see whereupon you cast your eye!" Mr. Ainsel rubbed his hands together, then snatched up the bracelet. On closer inspection it looked genuine, and far too valuable to languish in an undifferentiated heap. "Yuletide is upon us. Perhaps a certain young lady might appreciate the gesture?"

Ben tried to imagine Lady Juliet's reaction to such a gift. He could give it a polish, place it in a handsome box with a red velvet interior....

But what sort of message would that send? An extravagant

Christmas present, mere days after her public reconciliation with her ne'er-do-well husband? He shook his head. "I'm afraid not."

Mrs. Parry made a shocked noise. "Oh, Dr. Bones, for shame. I have no doubt Miss Jenkins would adore it. Golden roses for a Rose."

"Er... well...." Ben stammered, unable to come up with a neutral reply. He'd walked out with Miss Rose Jenkins a few times, which the village folk seemed to think equivalent to calling the banns. She was very pretty, extremely petite, and made for amiable company, deferring to his wishes and agreeing with everything he said. Many men would had called Rose the ideal woman, and in some ways Ben agreed—except when she wasn't standing in front of him, he tended to forget her existence.

"But listen to me, selling you short," Mrs. Parry said. "Poor Dr. Bones has already selected something extraordinary for Miss Jenkins, and he daren't breathe a word, for fear of spoiling the surprise. The ladies at Morton's guessed as much, and I see now they were right."

Ben, who until that moment hadn't realized the village had formed a public expectation on that score, could only hope the gift he'd actually bought Rose—a picture frame—wouldn't get him run out of Birdswing on a rail.

"No to the bracelet, then?" Mr. Ainsel tossed it back in the chest. Thrusting his hands into the heap, he rooted around with blithe disregard for the delicate items, churning up more curios: a silver cigarette case, opera glasses, a silk glove, and what looked to Ben like a yellow-brown human jaw bone, complete with teeth.

"What's that?" he said, meaning the jaw bone, but it had already disappeared beneath a knot of ribbons and pearls. Mr. Ainsel's deft little hands reached in that direction, but plucked out something else instead.

"Here's a pretty thing. Very clever," the shopkeeper said, wrinkles stacking up as he grinned. "If you lose your way, I say, seek the North Star and you'll go far. And if the heavens are hidden from your sight, carry a pocket star." He passed the object to Ben.

"A pocket compass," Ben said. He'd had one as a boy, but not like this. The compass was an antique, at least fifty years old, perhaps a hundred. Palm-sized and made of brass, it rested in a shagreen case with a tiny latch.

"Made by Dolland of London, as you see inscribed on the face," Mr. Ainsel said. "Its lodestone is magnetite. The housing is called a binnacle. On rough seas, even a good compass may fail to point you to True North, without a binnacle to hold it steady."

Ben studied the compass, delighted. Some old-fashioned scientific instruments, like astrolabes and brass microscopes, were practically works of art, and the compass was no exception. "How much?"

"A double denarius."

"I'm sorry?"

"A francorum rex?"

"I don't—"

"Thruppence-ha'penny?"

Ben stared at the little man. "You can't be serious. This must be worth ten pounds at least."

Mr. Ainsel sighed. "You drive a hard bargain, sir," he said dramatically. "In this case, you're determined to drive the price *up*, it seems, but I've never cared much for coin. I'd rather have your promise."

The hair on the back of Ben's neck stood up. For the first time he realized the little man in the emerald green coat had bilateral postaxial polydactyly—an extra finger on each hand.

"A promise!" Mrs. Parry repeated. Unlike Ben, she seemed charmed by the notion. "What sort of promise?"

"Nothing terrible. No first born sons or prize milk cows. I've enough of both to last ten lifetimes," Mr. Ainsel said lightly. He clasped his hands behind his back and put on a smile. His gaze, however, was serious. "I'll gladly give you this antique nautical compass, once the possession of a very fine gentleman, in exchange for this: you must promise that the next time someone makes a wish, you will grant it."

It might have been twenty years since Ben took a fairy story seriously, but such lessons of boyhood endured.

11

"I won't make a bargain like that." He thrust the wonderful old compass in its cunning shagreen case back at Mr. Ainsel. "Most people wish for things I can't grant, like a quick end to the war. Or a cure that hasn't been invented yet. And some wishes aren't very nice. Suppose I overhear Mrs. Archer wishing ARP Warden Gaston dead again?"

"She does fantasize about that sort of thing more than she should." Mrs. Parry tutted. "I myself try not to wish him dead more than once a week."

Hands still clasped behind his back, Mr. Ainsel laughed. It sounded joyful rather than cynical; more of wisdom than connivance.

"I'm not trying to trick you, Dr. Bones. Only to arrange a bit of kindness in a world that grows unkinder by the day," he said. "It's Yule. Christmas. *Joyeux Noël.* Nothing would please me more than to give you that compass. All I ask in return is that you give something to the next person who needs it. I'm not trying to dupe you into doing mischief, much less murder. If someone makes a wish in your presence during this most felicitous of seasons, I'd like you to grant it. Or at least give your all in the trying."

"That sounds reasonable," Mrs. Parry said.

"Oh, it is, I assure you." Mr. Ainsel dug into the chest one more time, coming up with something in the palm of his hand. "And if Dr. Bones will give me his solemn oath, I'll throw in—this!"

"A mermaid," Mrs. Parry breathed, eyes wide like a little girl's. Accepting the porcelain figurine, she brought it to the counter lamp for a better look. "It's perfect. Painted with such skill. Blonde hair, red lips, and a blue-green tail. You couldn't have chosen a better mermaid if you molded her from my dreams."

"Well?" Mr. Ainsel asked Ben.

From the expression on Mrs. Parry's face, nothing and no one could have parted her from that porcelain mermaid. If Ben declined to promise, and Mr. Ainsel refused to accept more traditional remuneration, his sweet busybody of a neighbor was liable to turn thief.

"Fine," Ben said. "I promise. But only—"

"Done," the little man cried, hoisting the chest like it weighed nothing and propelling it back behind the flimsy curtains with remarkable speed. "Done and done and done, as they say. There's no 'but only' after the words 'I promise!'" Hurrying to the door, he threw it open.

Colder than ever, the wind rushed in. Above Ben's head, the detritus in the rafters swung alarmingly, especially the battered old sled. The paraffin lamps on the counter snuffed in unison, which was as fortunate as it was strange, because it was full dark outside. The blackout was in effect from sunset to sunrise. That meant all lights out-of-doors were forbidden, lest German bombers use such beacons to attack England with greater precision.

"My goodness, I had no idea it was so late," Mrs. Parry said. "The lights went out so quick, I can't see a thing."

"Nor I. Take my arm." Shifting his grasp on the heavy brass compass, Ben used his cane to feel ahead of them, getting them past the tables and out the door. He expected to find Mr. Ainsel in the street, and intended to give him a few choice words about common courtesy, but the little man in the emerald coat was nowhere to be seen.

"Stay with me, please, while my eyes adjust," Mrs. Parry said, clutching Ben's arm. "I've never been so far from home during the blackout. I'm afraid I'll be run down in the street."

Ben, who actually had been run down in the street, and had the limp to prove it, patted his neighbor reassuringly. "Don't be afraid. We're going the same direction, remember? I'll be with you every step of the way."

He glanced over his shoulder, wondering again where Mr. Ainsel had buggered off to, and saw the door to Howell's Nonesuch was shut. The picture window was dark, the heavy blackout curtains in place. Somehow the little man had scampered back inside and closed up the shop without making a peep.

"Mr. Ainsel was an odd duck, wasn't he?" Mrs. Parry said as they made their way home under a starless sky. "Mr. Howell is a bit dull, and rarely has anything worthwhile on offer, but there's something to be said for a reassuring manner. Do you suppose we'll ever see that little man again?"

If I don't keep my promise, Ben thought with a prickle of unease, *I suppose I just might.*

Chapter Two

"Ow!" cried Juliet Linton-Bolivar.

"That didn't hurt," said Dinah, who had recently been promoted against her will—and Juliet's—to the old-fashioned position of lady's maid.

"I beg your pardon." Juliet turned away from the vanity to look at Dinah, who stood behind her with hair brush in hand. "How on earth are you able to ascertain what the individual nerve endings in my scalp do and do not feel?"

"I barely touched you. Lady Victoria gave me this brush. It's the same one she used on your hair when you were a baby." Dinah's tone, like her expression, was colorless. A whey-faced, freckled girl of sixteen, she'd joined the staff of Belsham Manor after her mother died. The maids and cooks enjoyed an easy camaraderie, especially now that the much-feared housekeeper, Mrs. Locke, had been discharged. But Dinah, Mrs. Locke's former whipping girl, remained withdrawn. She rarely spoke, and what little she did say tended to be unhelpful, if not downright sullen.

Fingering the tortoiseshell brush's extra soft bristles, she added, "I don't like this any better than you do. But Lady Victoria was quite firm. Milady."

"Well. My goodness, Dinah. From you, that counts as a virtual soliloquy."

Dinah froze. Juliet had seen that look before, on the faces of certain crofter's children. It was the look of one who'd been taught from birth that saying the wrong thing would be answered with a slap, a punch, or worse.

"A soliloquy," Juliet explained gently, "is just another word for speech. Monologue. An uninterrupted address of some length involving multiple words. You've been exposed to soliloquies before, have you not? During a church play or pantomime, perhaps?"

"Yes, milady. But not in church. Only from you, milady."

Thank heavens Ben isn't here, Juliet thought. *He'd tease me mercilessly.*

Of course, it was rather silly to imagine Dr. Bones in her bedroom. It was a place he had no business visiting, especially now that she'd been forced into a sham reconciliation with Ethan. But her heart was stubborn, and her last encounter with Ben had taught it to hope.

"Yes, you're quite right, I do speak in soliloquies from time to time," Juliet said briskly. "After so many years without intelligent discourse, I learned to generate my own. As for the word 'milady,' I'd prefer if you jettisoned it. Too many honorifics before dinner spoils my digestion. Now. Let's get on, shall we?"

"Yes, mi—yes."

Juliet faced the mirror again, forcing herself to watch as Dinah brushed her hair. The new color, honey-blonde, and the new cut, a bob that could be smartened up with pin curls or a jeweled barrette, was still strange to her. For the first couple of days she'd literally jumped whenever she passed a mirror and glimpsed a towering woman with cinema-star hair.

Her deep blue dress suited her better than any she'd ever owned. The dressmaker, whom Lady Victoria had brought in from Paris, had "a gift for draping stupendous women," as he'd announced with a heavy French accent. Each bespoke creation emphasized her waist— or, more accurately, made it look like she had one—while turning her broad shoulders and long legs into assets. Allowing her still-lovely, ever-stylish mother to reinvent her had made Juliet feel attractive for the first time in her life.

Then there was Ben's reaction. When he'd looked upon the "new" Juliet for the first time, staring unabashedly and at a loss for words, she'd felt more than attractive—she'd felt pretty. Not as pretty as Rose Jenkins, of course, but pretty enough for him, which was all she'd ever wanted.

Unfortunately, the old Juliet had never learned to do anything with her limp brown hair except scrape it back into an unflattering bun. A short hair style required careful preparation. The old Juliet had treated her clothes, mostly bought from the men's section of mail-order catalogs, with the same degree of care she accorded flour sacks. Fine fabrics with delicate zips and laces would be ruined if treated that way. The old Juliet never wore makeup—it seemed like a mine-field—and was even shy about choosing her own accessories, particularly hats.

That was where Dinah came in. Lady Victoria had decreed Dinah would assist Juliet until she was sufficiently comfortable maintaining her new look on her own.

"Very well. Recommence the brushing and styling," Juliet said. "I'll endeavor to behave. And if we're going to be a team, we really must get to know one another better. How about a round of Impertinent Questions?"

"I don't know how to play," Dinah said. Her reflection in the mirror looked wary.

Juliet didn't know how to play, either, as she had only just made up the game. That didn't stop her from delineating the rules with great authority.

"It's simple. Two women play in secret. They agree, under pain of death—"

"Death?"

Sometimes Juliet forgot how very childlike Dinah was under that sullen shell. "Very well, not death. Under pain of inconvenience, they agree to never repeat anything said during the game. Mutual trust is essential."

Dinah continued brushing Juliet's hair, watching her face in the mirror.

"We take turns asking one another impertinent questions," Juliet said. "Whatever the question is, it *must* be answered. You can say pass only once. If you pass twice, you lose."

"I have a feeling I'll say pass twice," Dinah said. "Best not to play."

"But wait. The game is played for stakes as well as bragging rights. We must each ante up. The offering needn't be material. But it must be satisfactory to each woman. In my case," Juliet said, reaching for a jeweled pin she'd seen Dinah admire, "I shall put up this pin. If your questions are so impertinent that you force me to say pass twice, it's yours."

Dinah goggled at the pin. It was actually quite lovely—gold and garnets, perfect for Christmastime.

"I'd like to win," she breathed. "But what could I put up? You have everything."

"Nonsense," Juliet said. "I have no one to help me deliver meals to the shut-ins this week. Another pair of hands—cheerful hands, connected to a dutiful body and a smiling face—would be much appreciated. Agreed? Capital! I shall issue the first query. Please recall the name of the game is Impertinent Questions, not Meek Chatter for Ninnies."

"I'm ready," Dinah said, switching on that what-is-this-world-coming-to device Lady Victoria had bought on a hairdresser's recommendation: the self-heating electric curling rod. It looked harmless enough, sitting in its ceramic cradle, but it went from cool to warm to volcanic so fast, Juliet had learned to guard against sudden movements. She'd already singed off a patch of arm hair, thanks to a grandiose gesture.

"Very well, Dinah. They say you're an orphan. Is that true? Have you any living relatives?"

"One."

Juliet waited eagerly. Nothing else was forthcoming.

"Yes, well, that's a start. Perhaps I should write what constitutes an acceptable answer into the game's bylaws. The answer cannot be yes or no. And it must possess a certain revelatory quality."

"What?"

"It has to be worth hearing. These living relatives of yours. Who are they?"

"I have a brother. He was a Borstal boy. Never heard from again, but he used to say he'd run away to New Zealand. Maybe he did," Dinah said. "There's my dad's mum. She might be living. Dad said she used to go from pub to pub, game for anything. Only the good die young."

"I abhor that particular saying," Juliet said.

"I don't." Dinah held her palm over the electric rod to gauge its warmth. "It means my mum was good."

Juliet felt fortunate to be sitting in front of a mirror. It reminded her to arrest the look of horror creeping over her face, and replace it with something that Dinah wouldn't mistake for condescension. "How sad about your mother. And how did you lose your father?"

"He buggered off when we needed him most." Dinah wrapped one of Juliet's tresses around the rod. "Is it my turn to ask a question?"

Juliet nodded, and gasped.

"Don't! I could burn your scalp. Er, right. My question." Dinah took a deep breath. "Why are you pretending to take Mr. Bolivar back?"

"Good God!"

"You did say this isn't Meek Chatter for Ninnies." Dinah's eyes glinted. Life hadn't kicked all the spirit out of her yet.

19

"Yes, well, when it comes to Impertinent Questions, you've proven yourself a prodigy. Here is my answer: pass." Juliet sat quietly as Dinah unspooled a perfect blonde curl. When the next tress was safely wrapped, she said, "And here is my second question. If you could snap your fingers and be anything in the world, what would you be?"

"Some man's wife."

"Yes, of course, that's a given. I mean you. Personally."

"A lady's maid."

Juliet groaned. "We aren't playing Obsequious Replies. Tell me the truth or pass."

It took Dinah a few moments to muster an answer. "I'd be in charge of the WI."

"The Women's Institute? Why?"

"Because when those ladies speak at the podium, everyone listens."

Juliet filed that away for future rumination. "Well done. Your turn."

"Are you in love with Dr. Bones?"

It was perhaps fortunate that the question was posed when Juliet had a hot steel rod to her head, or she might have spoilt everything with an accusatory outburst. Allowing Dinah to unspool that curl and wrap the next tress gave Juliet time to remember two things. First, she herself had proposed the game and made the rules. Second, Dinah was clearly more perceptive than her colorless façade suggested. She'd put her finger on the question Juliet most wanted to be asked—a truth that came clear only after it was spoken aloud.

"Once again, Dinah, I must say well done. At this time, I can do nothing but pass. Therefore, the game is done and the pin is yours."

Dinah squealed. It was the first time Juliet had heard the girl emit such a joyous sound, making the entire experience worthwhile.

"That was an agreeable way to pass a quarter-hour," Juliet said. "But now I'm famished. How much more frippery must I endure before I'm permitted to show my face at dinner?"

"Three curls on the other side for balance. Powder, lipstick, and mascara. Then you can go downstairs to Lady Victoria and Mr. Bolivar." Dinah spoke more easily; playing Impertinent Questions had loosened her tongue. "You said, 'at this time.'"

"Beg pardon?"

"At this time," Dinah repeated, unwinding another curl. "Does that mean if I ask about Dr. Bones the next time we play, you might answer?"

Juliet pondered the question seriously. Two people knew of her feelings for Ben. One was her mother, Lady Victoria. The other was Ethan Bolivar, the man whom she could no longer think of as her husband, not even in jest. Both had guessed the truth; it appeared that Dinah had, too. How lovely it would be to talk about Ben, to share her hopes and frustrations with someone other than her mare, Epona, who hardly seemed interested.

Of course, as Father Cotterill liked to point out, "the birds sing in Birdswing," which meant that in their village, twittering gossips were legion. Confiding in Dinah might be foolish. Then again, Dinah had recently been at Juliet's mercy over the kind of secret that occasionally drove women to throw themselves off bridges, visit back alleys, or disappear. In Dinah's case, the baby had been discreetly adopted, giving them both a second chance at life. Juliet had never breathed a word, and she never would.

"I can't explain about Mr. Bolivar," Juliet said. "By that I mean, I am quite literally prohibited from discussing the matter. Believe my motives to be noble, for they are. Certainly they have nothing to do with—" She cut her eyes toward the elephant in the room, the enormous Linton heirloom bed. "I sleep alone, as you've apparently guessed. Beyond that, please don't ask about Mr. Bolivar. But Dr. Bones ...." She smiled at herself in the mirror. "Dr. Bones is fair game."

Chapter Three

Letty Smith lived on Pigmeadow Lane, in what had once been the most disgraceful dwelling in Birdswing. Called the Crow's Hut, it was the last surviving remnant of that loose collection of "nooks, crannies, thieves, and grannies" that made up Old Crow village. Respectable hamlets, like the neighboring village of Barking, still bore the traces of their medieval forbearers. In such pedigreed villages, even after fire, flood, or rapacious progress took its toll, any amateur historian could tell where the castle had been, where the sixteenth century market had stood, et cetera. Birdswing was different.

Until the newly-created Sir Thaddeus Linton arrived around 1840, Old Crow was a conglomeration of shacks, back-to-backs, hide-aways, and unlicensed watering holes. It seemed to have no working population, only miscreants on the lam and old women whom no one wanted. Some were sharp-tongued widows. Some kept too many cats. One was said to be a witch. She'd built the Crow's Hut herself, so the story went, which accounted for why the Council declared it a public nuisance by 1932. The undressed stone walls were sturdy enough, but the much-mended tin roof (really just a collection of shipyard metal cobbled together) and grease paper windows were more than Lady Victoria could bear.

Over the vigorous objections of Letty, who could still walk in those days, if she used two canes and took it slowly, Lady Victoria had hired men to replace the rusted tin with a shingled roof. A week later she'd sent them back to replace the paper windows with shutters. The Crow's Hut was still technically in violation of certain Council resolutions, including minimum number of rooms (it had only one) and plumbing (it had none, only an outhouse and a hand pump, both located in the back garden). But compromise was the essence of any community, and Letty was something of a Birdswing institution. If they forced her out of her home, where would she go? The work-houses were shut down, thankfully, and pensioner's homes were open only to a few.

"Come in! It's a foul weather day, Dr. Bones," Letty called in answer to his knock. "Storm's rolling in. Nothing for me to do but hold fast."

Letty's bed was located beside the cast iron stove. Kindhearted villagers had provided pillows, a patchwork quilt, and a bedside table. Her cup and water jug had been pushed aside in favor of Mrs. Parry's mermaid.

"Isn't she beautiful?" Letty asked. "Presents should wait until Christmas Eve, of course, but dear Edwina wanted me to have her right away. Mind my feet, Doctor," she added, as Ben opened his bag and put on his stethoscope. "Can't even bear a coverlet against them this morning."

"So I see," Ben said. The patchwork quilt was pulled up to Letty's chin, but her lower legs stuck out like raw red sticks. Her knees were inflated, as always, and her bony feet hurt to look at. The great toes were twice the size they should have been, the smaller toes frozen with unnatural bends. There was only one effective treatment for rheumatoid arthritis, a combination of aspirin and bedrest, and for Letty, neither did much. In the big cities there were clinics that would gladly inject patients with gold, irrigate their colons, vaccinate them with viral combinations or attempt to exercise them into remission, but Ben viewed all such treatments with skepticism. Besides, Letty could barely make it from The Crow's Hut to St. Mark's for the yearly Easter service, much less hop a train to London.

He went through the motions of an exam, but nothing had changed, which was probably as much as he could hope for. Letty *looked* better, and that in itself was a victory. Her gaunt face was haunted by the ghost of prettiness; the deep lines, white hair, and missing teeth didn't eradicate the symmetry of her features or the sweetness of her smile.

Having taken her pulse, listened to her lungs, assessed her joints and asked the usual questions, Ben pulled up a chair for the heart of his visit. There was only one thing she needed that he could actually give her, and while it was time-consuming, it was not difficult.

"Where were we?" she asked, picking up the porcelain mermaid and turning it over in her hands. "The Mermaid of Padstow?"

"We finished that."

"Ah. The Mermaid of Zennor, then," Letty said. "A bard carries tales for all places and all sorts. I learnt tales of giants and wights for the kiddies, because they like things what go bump in the night. I learnt stories of doomed romance for the ladies, and tales of adventure for the gents. But I had it wrong. In the pubs, the ladies let down their hair. They want bawdy stories and jokes. It's the fishermen in their cups who like pining hearts and doomed romance." She chuckled. "Can you picture it? Beefy blokes who swilled rum like water fell dead quiet for mermaids and magic and hopeless love."

Ben made a noncommittal noise. Letty seemed to catch that. There was very little she didn't catch.

"Lucky for you, this one contains a bit of hope." Her eyes sparkled. "Do you know St. Senara's church? It stands on a green hill overlooking the sea. Once upon a time, St. Senara's had a very impressive vicar. He preached against worldliness and wickedness, as vicars do. He thought his wisdom pulled in the people each Sunday, but it didn't. They came to hear the choir's angelic voices. Whether their songs of praise carried on the wind up to Heaven, I know not," Letty said, falling into a storyteller's cadence. "But their sweet voices fell upon the waves and drifted down to Neptune's kingdom, where mermen rule and sailors sleep.

"The finest voice of St. Senara's choir belonged to the vicar's son, a lad named Matthew. He was a pretty one. Deep blue eyes that made the girls whisper. Brown hair with just a glimmer of ginger. A noble brow, and a smile like sorcery."

Ben chuckled. Letty always found a way to flatter him in the course of her stories. It would have been churlish of him to object.

"In the Advent season, the hymnal was opened to songs about Mary and the birth of Christ. Throughout Zennor, villagers hung the mistletoe and the Christmas bush. They made up their fire with fragrant branches, burned the block, and asked me for tales of the Three Wise Men and Father Christmas...."

"The block?" Ben interrupted.

"Some call it the Yule log. But in Kernow we've always called it the burning of the block, just as we've always hung the bush and danced beneath it. You *do* know what I mean by the Christmas bush?"

"My housekeeper educated me," Ben said. Mrs. Cobblepot, who kept many Pagan customs of the south west country, had constructed two such "bushes," or traditional wreaths, out of holly, ivy, and mistletoe woven through a withy frame. One bush hung in Ben's front room; the other was displayed in his examining room, to the praise and delight of his patients. During a wartime Christmas, the blackout made caroling by candlelight or lighting a tree on the village green illegal, so indoor observances were all the more meaningful.

"One Sunday at dusk, a woman no one had ever seen entered St. Senara's church and slipped into a pew. She was neither young nor old, but beautiful and ageless, as if carven from stone. Her eyes were a clear blue-green, like the water at St. Ives, and her black hair fell in ringlets down her back. She carried herself with the bearing of a queen, looking neither left nor right, but only at the choir, and only at Matthew.

"After the evening service, most of the villagers filed back to their homes, to finish the Sabbath in quiet prayer, as was their way. A few rogues filed back to the pub, to finish the Sabbath with a pint of ale, as was my way," she added, laughing. "To the vicar's displeasure, his son Matthew followed the strange woman to the pub. There he spent the rest of the night in her company, drinking and boasting while she looked on, combing her hair.

"The next day, the vicar rebuked his son," Letty went on. "He told Matthew that the woman was clearly a mermaid, and mermaids were agents of sin. 'The wages of sin are death,' the vicar warned. He reminded Matthew that when the siren beckons and the man follows, he's pulled beneath the waters and never seen again. But Matthew's ears were filled with the song of the sea, and when do the young ever listen to the old in matters of the heart? He paid no heed, even as his father called her a temptress, a seductress, and a lie masquerading as a woman."

"I like her already," Lady Juliet called, entering. Her maid, Dinah, followed with a hamper on her arm. "Forgive me for barging in, and do continue. Dinah, put the basket on that table. We'll listen to the end of the story before we unpack Mrs. Smith's dinner."

"Gather round and be welcome," Letty said, perking up at the arrival of more listeners. Her sharp eyes roved curiously over Dinah.

"Hallo, Lady Juliet."

"Hallo, Dr. Bones."

He tried to maintain eye contact, but she looked away. How could he ease the discomfort between them? He wasn't meant to know the truth about her and Ethan. And she was so changed, it was hard to keep from staring. He wanted to touch her face, run his fingers through her hair, tease her like he used to. Well—not quite like he used to. Before, his motive had been to make her laugh and amuse himself. Now he wanted to impress her, see what sort of battle lines she would draw, and try to cross them.

Dinah dragged a pouf to the bedside. As Juliet settled herself on a stool, Ben watched from the corner of his eye. She sat taller these days. He liked that.

"Where was I?" Letty asked. "Oh, aye—the mysterious lady who visited Zennor. When the sun rose on Monday, she was nowhere to be found. It wasn't till the next Sunday, which was Christmas Eve, that she returned. Now the villagers knew she was surely a mermaid, so they gawped as she entered St. Senara's, trying to see the bewitched legs beneath her skirt."

Dinah, who'd been helplessly staring at Letty's exposed legs and feet, gulped and looked away. Letty laughed.

"Look all you want. I only wish I had a fish tail," she said, smiling. "As before, the choir sang, and Matthew's voice was wondrous to hear. He'd never looked more handsome. And as before, when the service ended, the villagers filed away to their homes, but Matthew disappeared with the lady on his arm.

"The vicar could have pleaded with his son," Letty said, looking at Dinah. "He could have asked him to stay, not out of fear, but in the name of love. Do you think he did?"

Dinah shook her head.

"No, indeed. Drunk on his rectitude, the vicar disowned his son, saying he could not sing again in St. Senara's choir until he renounced the mermaid and all appearance of sin.

"But time has a way of softening even the proudest heart. On Christmas morning, the vicar resolved to make it up with his son. To preach about forgiveness and let the boy sing. But Matthew had disappeared. His father and the villagers searched everywhere. Throughout the winter they scoured the cliffs and the beach of Zennor, but no trace of Matthew was ever found. Still, on clear nights, some hear a man's beautiful voice carried on the waves, singing to the mermaid who pulled him under the sea. Sometimes what we call wickedness is true love."

Lady Juliet snorted.

"Quiet, you." As a Birdswing institution, Letty spoke to Lady

Juliet however she pleased. Lady Juliet never complained. In fact, from what Ben could see, she enjoyed it.

"Love is mysterious, my girl," Letty told Dinah. "Oft-times we are too wrapped up in our little customs and rules to recognize love, even at this time of year. Do you believe it?"

Dinah nodded eagerly.

She was still a child in many ways, Ben realized. Though she'd had an affair, been deserted, and given her out-of-wedlock baby to adoptive parents, withstanding those events didn't necessarily guarantee emotional growth. Dinah's stoicism often gave the illusion of maturity. Now he saw her as she really was: a sixteen-year-old captivated by a Cornish fairy tale.

"The vicar was grief-stricken," Letty said, taking up the tale again. "How he wished he'd tried to reconcile with his son on Christmas Eve when he had the chance. He bitterly regretted condemning the lady without even trying to know her, so he decided to offer an olive branch.

"Remember how I told you when the lady visited St. Senara's, she sat in the same pew twice? Well, the vicar paid homage to her choice. He carved the image of a mermaid into the pew. She was depicted in the classic style, naked and beautiful with a curved fish tail. A mirror in one hand and a comb in the other. Many assumed the vicar was playing a trick. Trying to lure her back on land to admire her portrait, as mermaids are known to be vain.

"But in truth, the vicar wanted nothing but a second chance to beg his son's forgiveness." A tear slipped down Letty's cheek. "The Mermaid of Zennor is lovely. You can enter St. Senara's to this day and see her image for yourself. But the vicar's olive branch wasn't accepted. He died alone. His son never returned." Voice cracking on the last word, she covered her face with her hands and sobbed.

"Letty, are you quite all right?" Lady Juliet asked.

"Are you in pain?" Ben had heard Letty spin many tales, but she'd never broken down this way, no matter how sad the ending.

"Should I fetch a mug down to the Sheared Sheep for you, Mrs. Smith?" Dinah asked. "Bring you back some cider?"

Letty wiped her eyes with her sleeve. "Does my doctor object?"

"Not at all," Ben said.

"If it's not too much trouble," Letty said weakly. "Perhaps you could fetch me back Guinness... for strength...."

Dinah glanced at Lady Juliet, who seemed to bite back a laugh. Reaching into her purse, she brought out a coin and passed it to the maid. Clearly Letty wasn't too distraught to beg a taste of the good stuff.

"Sorry, my loves," she said as Dinah carried her glass mug into the yard to wash it out under the pump. "I don't know why I let myself be overcome. Well—I do. Forget that rosy rubbish I fed the girl. Christmas is all about the letdown."

"I feel the same at times," Ben said, examining the porcelain mermaid. "But Mrs. Parry was steadfast in her determination to get you this. And that's something, isn't it? A very old friend who knows you so well?"

"I'm off," Dinah called from the yard.

With the young woman absent, Ben felt free to ask, "What's the significance of the mermaid? Mrs. Parry said you had to have it, or she feared for your life."

"Clearly, it's a link to Letty's past," Lady Juliet announced. As a passionate admirer of Dr. Carl Jung, she was familiar with the tenets of psychoanalysis, occasionally going so far as to diagnose people who were within earshot. "A mermaid carries hidden psychological meaning. It symbolizes the free-spirited woman, who can travel at will and ignore the laws of polite society. Much as you did in your youth."

"So I did," Letty agreed without much enthusiasm. Ben and Lady Juliet exchanged glances. Clearly, the mermaid wasn't simply a remembrance of her younger days.

"Speaking of ignoring the laws of polite society," Lady Juliet said. "Surely you've proven your independence by squatting in this wretched hole long enough."

Letty sucked in her breath, eyes flashing.

"Perhaps now isn't the time—" Ben began, but Lady Juliet would have none of it.

"When is the time? When the poor woman lies comatose? Letty, we just sent Dinah outside to the pump next to your privy to wash out a mug in cold water. It's quite selfish of you to live this way, knowing how it worries my mother. Allow me to send for plumbers. You can embark on 1940 with hot and cold taps, a kitchen sink, and a W.C. instead of a soup tureen under the bed."

"I won't be embarking on 1940," Letty said stubbornly, taking the mermaid from Ben and tracing its face with a trembling finger. "I'm not strong enough to make the trip to Plymouth. Wasn't strong enough last year, either. Time to pack it in."

"Right! Perfect," Lady Juliet declared. "Since you plan to expire in a matter of weeks, you can have no objection to me getting the plumbers round. Mother will be over the moon. As for making your yearly trip to Plymouth, I should think that if you'll put off meeting your maker, another chance will come before you know it."

"What's this about Plymouth?" Ben asked.

"She knows." Letty pointed at Lady Juliet.

"I know far less than I'd like," she admitted. "I know that each winter, you take the train to Plymouth sometime after All Saints Day and don't return for a day or so. It seems like something of a ritual. I've seen you go bedecked like a duchess, and come back weighed down with presents for the village. I've seen you go on two canes, your coat buttoned over a house dress, and come back on a stretcher, down for the count till spring. But I've never known why. The rumor used to be, your *amour* lived in the Barbican."

"So to speak." Letty sat up straighter. It seemed after sobbing, asking for Guinness, and threatening to die, she was ready to talk about what was really on her mind. "It's my boy, Jacky."

"Your son lives in Plymouth?" Ben remembered what Mrs. Parry had said about the dark-eyed baby Letty had brought with her to Birdswing.

31

"He's buried in the Stonehouse cemetery. That is to say, his name is carved on a plaque there, next to the names of six other fishermen. They were lost at sea in the month of December."

"I'm sorry to hear that," Ben said. He glanced at Lady Juliet, but she avoided his eye. That was what frustrated him the most, being out of sync with her. From the moment they'd met, they'd clashed, critiqued one another, and teased one another, but they'd always known themselves to be on the same team. Now their pieces had been dragged to the board's starting line, and neither would advance until one of them was willing to throw the dice.

"I'd like to hear about Jacky. What about you, Lady Juliet?" he asked, touching her shoulder.

"I—I'd like that, too." Her gaze fluttered down, held there for a moment, then darted back up to see if he was still looking. When he smiled, an encouraging blush crept up her cheek.

"Jacky was a sweet baby and a good boy," Letty said fondly. "Never a cross word to me, and no more mischief than usual. Handsome, like his father, but kindly, like my old dad, thank the Lord. He was twenty-two when he was called to Glory. Bad enough to lose him so young. But on the day his boat was lost, we hadn't spoken for a year."

"Someone told me you fell out when he went to sea," Lady Juliet said.

"I wasn't happy about it," Letty admitted, shifting under the covers in what looked like a vain attempt to get comfortable. "I wanted to keep him close, in Birdswing. But he heard the call of the sea. Apprenticed on a schooner out of Plymouth. There he met a girl on the docks—you can imagine the sort. People thought me rough and common as fleas, spinning tales in pubs and drifting from village to village. But I was a bard, not one of those dock girls.

"How I despised them," she went on. "Forever fiddling with their hair, checking their lipstick in a mirror, calling and waving to sailors. Bad enough that Jacky chose to walk out with such a— a person. When he told me they were to be wed, I forbid it."

"I suppose any mum would have done the same," Ben said.

"Oh, yes, I had God on my side," Letty agreed. "Or so I thought. She was a hussy at best, an out-and-out harlot at worst. Not that Jacky listened to my opinion. He stood up with her that Sunday next. I didn't go. And when he brought her round to this very doorstep, I refused to open the door. That was the last time I saw him. Watching from my window as he walked away.

"At the time I was quite pleased with myself. I wanted my son to suffer in silence. To eat his heart out, and leave her in due course, just like his father left me. Aren't we perverse, the way we try to alleviate our suffering by transferring it to others? I see now, it wasn't for me to judge Jacky's wife. All I was meant to do was offer kindness and understanding. I gave them neither."

"He knew you loved him," Ben said firmly.

"No son doubts his mother's love," Lady Juliet agreed.

"Oh, yes, lift the mad old bat's spirits." Letty laughed, picking up the porcelain mermaid again. "Every year since Jacky was lost, I carry an image of the Mermaid of Zennor to Plymouth and give it to the sea. A sketch, a watercolor, a toy. It's daft, I know. But it's only through stories that I understand the world. The vicar wanted to make peace with the siren who took his son. So do I."

"How many years since Jacky was lost?" Ben asked.

"Seventeen."

"Well. This is none of my business, of course, but have you tried to trace his widow? After so long, she might welcome the chance to know you. Perhaps there's even a grandchild."

"I don't have to trace her. She's with him." Letty sighed.

Ben and Lady Juliet exchanged glances again. "You mean she was on the ship when it went down?"

"No. A month after his ship went down, she walked to the cliffs and threw herself into Jennycliff Bay. Some picnickers saw her fall. She didn't surface. Her body never washed ashore." Letty put the mermaid back on her nightstand. "Those first years, I journeyed to Plymouth in memory of my boy. Now, I journey in memory of her,

33

too. Toward the end, the trip hurt me in body as well as soul, but I never let the pain win. Now, with my legs crippled and a war underway, I'm beaten. I wish...."

The words "I wish" fell on Ben with unexpected power. After reluctantly giving his promise to Mr. Ainsel, he'd put it out of his thoughts. Now it returned to him with fresh urgency. "You wish what?"

"I wish someone would go to Plymouth for me, and place the mermaid by Jacky's stone. Place it, and say a prayer that he forgives me—him and his wife."

Ben took a deep breath. He had neither the time nor the inclination. He'd certainly shaken off any childish fear of Mr. Ainsel and his Brothers Grimm-style bargain. But he could grant the wish, if he was willing to inconvenience himself.

"Right. I'll do it."

Eyes widening, Letty sat up taller in bed. "Dr. Bones, do you mean it? Don't tease a dying woman."

"You're not dying. And I'm not teasing. The trains will be booked with soldiers on leave and kiddies visiting their parents, but Plymouth isn't too far for me to drive," Ben said. Actually, the city was more than two hours away, and petrol was rationed. But as the physician responsible for a wide circle of the West Country, he got an extra share. "I'll go Sunday next."

"Sunday? But that's Christmas Eve."

"Not till sunset. And I'll be back before then," Ben said. "It's the only day besides Christmas itself that I have no patients booked. I'm happy to make the journey for you."

"Dr. Bones," Lady Juliet said, "you never fail to impress me."

"Don't puff up the poor man's ego," Letty said. "Someone must fetch me a map so I can draw him a route. Can't have him blundering all over Plymouth. Unless—you know Stonehouse graveyard, do you not, your ladyship?"

"Of course."

"Then you must go with Dr. Bones and guide him. Can't have

him getting trapped by the blackout, or he'll miss his first Christmas in Birdswing."

"You enjoy arranging other people's time, don't you?" Lady Juliet said.

"It's a privilege of the old to make demands on the young," Letty replied, unrepentant. "As a little girl, you always talked of traveling. Tramped over hill and dale with your old dad's compass. Now you can visit sweet Jacky's marker and place the mermaid where the water will take it."

"Where?" Ben asked.

"I don't know. I never know till I reach Plymouth, which I love almost as much as I love Birdswing," Letty said. "I'll want her lady-ship to bring me all the news. No offense, Dr. Bones, but young men can't be trusted for such tasks. They'll only say it was cold, or wet, or cloudy, or fair. I need someone to paint a picture in words, and that one is never short of words."

"*That one*," Lady Juliet said, raising an eyebrow, "hasn't agreed to accept this demand upon her time. I will, but only if you pay my price. You must agree to let me install modern plumbing. You've been in violation for years and the Council has overlooked the matter because you're a pillar of the community—"

"Pillar?" Letty laughed. "Pillock, more like."

"Be that as it may, only think how comfortable you'll be with hot and cold taps."

"I'm a dying woman," Letty insisted, face lighting up as Dinah reentered with a mug of Guinness in hand. "Step lively, girl, I've a powerful thirst. Oh. Yes, that's better," she said, drinking deeply. "But how can I cling to life while men with hammers and loud voices pull my house down around me?"

"I have the perfect solution," Lady Juliet said, pouncing. "You'll stay with Mother and me in Belsham Manor till the work is done."

Chapter Four

Juliet spent the next several days meddling in Letty's affairs and rearranging them to her satisfaction. The exercise not only played to her strengths, it kept her anticipation about the twenty-fourth of December to a manageable simmer. Allowing it to boil, to contemplate what amounted to an entire day with Ben and all the possibilities therein, rendered her useless in short order. But by the evening of the twenty-third, she'd run out of problems to solve. That meant the pot was on, the steam was billowing, and it was all she could do to sit still.

After dinner, she and her mother usually had drinks in the downstairs parlor. Lady Victoria liked what amounted to a thimbleful of brandy; Juliet preferred coffee, and plenty of it. Tonight, however, it merely exacerbated an ever-present stomach ache. Fortunately, their two very different houseguests were occupied elsewhere.

Ethan, who had been asked not to intrude on Juliet and her mother's private time, was down at the Sheared Sheep, probably holding court. The old men who made up its core clientele seemed to regard him as something of a conquering hero, which she would have found unbearable if it wasn't all for the greater good. Let them slap Ethan on the back and make lewd insinuations about how he'd supposedly put his wife in her place. This was Juliet's first wartime sacrifice, and it probably wouldn't be her last.

Letty, who would have been a welcome addition, had a standing invitation to join Juliet and Lady Victoria, but had thus far declined. She was on her feet again, albeit unsteadily, walking a few minutes each day with Dinah by her side. After an early dinner, she was too exhausted for anything but sleep.

As if reading Juliet's mind, Lady Victoria said, "You've worked a miracle on Letty. And by extension, Dinah. I quite enjoy seeing them together." Embroidery hoop on her lap, she was finishing up a Christmas present, something patriotic with the flags of Cornwall, England, and Great Britain.

"I can't take much credit. She gave in rather easily. Perhaps she's tired of living alone," Juliet said. "I never realized Dinah had the makings of a nurse."

"She's sympathetic, but not soft. She sees right through Letty's excuses," Lady Victoria said. "I overheard them this morning. I used to consider Dinah closemouthed, but with Letty she sounded quite spirited."

"You should hear her when she does my hair," Juliet said, recalling their game of Impertinent Questions.

"Speaking of your hair, it's lovely." Lady Victoria looked up from her embroidery with a smile. "Have you learned to do it yourself?"

"No. But I finished *The Buccaneers* and moved on to *The Code of the Woosters.*"

"That's probably a better use of your time. So. As you seem ready to launch out of that chair and fly around the room, I have to ask: Are you looking forward to tomorrow's excursion?"

Juliet didn't dare lock eyes with her mother, who saw too much. Settling for looking at something safer—three of the dogs, arranged by the hearth in a state of collapse—she said, "No doubt it will be jolly good."

Lady Victoria chuckled. "Poor Dr. Bones couldn't stop saying 'jolly good' after you and Ethan announced your so-called reconciliation, could he?"

"No. He sounded quite like a parrot with a concussion. It made me want to cry. I'm glad you can laugh at it."

"Forgive me. That was painful for you. Truth be told, it was painful for me, too." Lady Victoria put the hoop aside. "Though I've known for some time what he means to you, it wasn't until that moment that I realized what you meant to him."

"I wish I could believe that," Juliet said, startled. "But he wasn't gutted for long. After a day or two, it was back to business as usual."

"Yes, well, that's down to me," Lady Victoria said lightly. "I do regret leaving open the door to the back passage. Dr. Bones must have wandered all the way to the library. You and Ethan were conferring inside, and I fear whatever he overheard put him in the picture."

Juliet's gasp made one of the semi-comatose dogs twitch an ear. The "back passage," as she and her mother called it, was also known as "The Master's Way"—her ancestor Sir Thaddeus's grandiose name for Belsham Manor's hidden passage. It ran from the master bedroom to the library, and from the library to the dining room. Sir Thaddeus had used it to discreetly move his mistress to and fro. The staff used it as a cut-through, and Juliet used it when she couldn't sleep at night and needed a new book.

"Mother! What about the Official Secrets Act?" she cried, loud enough to be heard at the Ministry of Defense. Cringing, she added in a whisper, "They *hang* citizens who speak of what they know."

"Is that so?" Lady Victoria, who'd picked up the hoop again, didn't look up. "How fortunate for me, then, that I spoke not a word. True, I left a door open in my own home. Dr. Bones, being an investigator, investigated. You and Ethan were overheard, which is terribly unfortunate, but hardly criminal. Dr. Bones never questioned me afterward or acknowledged what happened in any way. But I was pleased to see him smile again, and stop lurching about like he wanted to hit something."

"You violated the spirit of the law."

"Did I? Good heavens. When the government starts hanging ladies of a certain age for violating the spirit of this or that, let me know. In the meantime, I'm quite pleased with how it all turned out. You were between Scylla and Charybdis. How could I sit by and watch as your future happiness was needlessly destroyed?"

"But it's not that simple," Juliet cried. The oldest dog lifted her head and whined.

"Oh, do be quiet, Florence. Talk about a dog's life. I should be so lucky, prone in front of a roaring fire, with nothing to do but luxuriate in the moment." Juliet sighed. "There I was, on the brink of freedom. Now I'm stuck acting the part of Ethan's wife for who knows how long. Ethan's *faithful* wife. Ben would have divorced Penny for adultery if she hadn't died first. The fact I'm still married is something he couldn't possibly overlook." She covered her face with her hands. "I can't believe I'm discussing this with my mother."

"Perhaps it's time you stopped thinking of me only as your mother," Lady Victoria said mildly. "There's so much we could share. But not if you cling to the role of a child."

"Are you saying... do you mean...?"

"I mean, things that are meant to happen will find a way, no matter what," Lady Victoria said. "Believe that, my darling, if you believe nothing else."

Chapter Five

Ben arrived at Belsham Manor just after breakfast. It was shaping up to be another gray day, bracingly cold, with a line of ragged clouds on the horizon. The morning air was clean and sweet, every breath like a draught of tonic. Sometimes when he took a big risk, he rushed toward it headlong, unsure of himself but carried along by pure speed, which made turning back impossible. Today was different. Today he was sure of himself—not of how it would all play out, of course, but of what he was risking, and why.

"Good morning," Ben called as the door opened and Lady Juliet emerged. Her smart black coat was buttoned up to her chin; her cloche was pulled low over her ears.

"Good morning to you," Ethan Bolivar said, appearing behind her. Tall and striking, he was still in his pajamas, dressing gown, and slippers. Famous for sleeping late, he'd apparently made a special effort to see her off. "You'll see her safely back before dark, I trust?"

"Ignore him," Lady Juliet commanded, hurrying down the marble steps without a backward glance. "Responding to his delusions will only reinforce them."

"She's in a vicious mood," Ethan said, grinning. "There's a café near Terulefoot that serves pie. I suggest you kip there if you want a pleasant journey." Waving, he stepped back inside and closed the door.

"You see what I must endure," she huffed, throwing herself into the passenger seat of Ben's Austin Ten. "They say virtue is its own reward, but I think it's shamelessness that really pays off. I feel like the ant in Aesop's fable. Except instead of smugly telling the grasshopper off, I'm forced to feed him, share my home with him, and listen to him play violin all winter long. *Poorly*," she added, as Ben got behind the wheel. "Why are you smiling?"

"Nothing. Only—it's quite nice to hear from the real Juliet. After listening to you play the dutiful wife for what felt like an eternity."

"Oh. Well. Yes. You see...."

"I know," he said.

"Mother told me you did. Just last night," she said, sounding like she might cry. "You can't imagine how desperately I've wanted to talk to you about it. I suppose here, in the car—"

"Let's not," he cut across her gently. "I won't have you breaking your oath on my account. I'm proud of you, if I'm being honest. You've convinced everyone that you and Ethan have truly reconciled. You even convinced me, for a little while."

She still looked close to tears, which wasn't remotely how Ben wanted the day to go. Time to change the subject.

"There's a woolen blanket in the back if you're cold," he said, starting the engine. "Mornings like these, I wish I had my dad's gas heater for the floorboards. It was bloody dangerous, but it kept our feet toasty."

"I'm fine. As navigator and first officer, as it were, of this expedition," she said, gaining confidence as she gave herself a promotion, "I prefer a little cold to keep my wits sharpened." Opening his glove box, she rummaged around, coming out with a map.

"Put that away. I know how to get to Plymouth."

"Yes, but can you find that café near Terulefoot? I think not.

Ethan is wrong about a great many things, but his advice about pie was spot-on." She shook out the accordion-folded map, which flapped into his sightline. He batted it aside.

"Navigator? I seem to recall a certain incident when you promised to direct me to Truro. We ended up on a narrow lane, boxed in by some especially belligerent sheep."

"That was down to you. You drive like a Londoner," Lady Juliet said. "Sheep can tell. They can look into a motorist's eye and winkle out the slightest trepidation."

The distance from Birdswing to Terulefoot melted away as the sun climbed and the sky went from gray to blue. Ben was surprised by how much he had to say, the sheer volume of conversation he'd apparently suppressed. At the café, he bought them each a slice of lattice-topped apple pie, hot out of the oven. They washed down the pie with glasses of milk.

"When it's time for lunch, it will be my treat," Lady Juliet said. They sat by the café's window, which offered a view of the hills and some black and white cows. "By the way, I have a terrible confession."

"You plan on ordering another piece of pie?"

"Worse. I didn't get you a Christmas present. Not because I didn't want to," she said. "Only because I wasn't sure you'd accept it."

Ben shrugged. "We're having a day out. We're having pie. What else could I ask for? Besides, I didn't get you anything, either. Not *per se*. But something Mrs. Smith said gave me a notion." Reaching into his coat pocket, he pulled out the antique compass.

"Happy Christmas," he said, placing it in front of her. "Sorry I didn't wrap it."

"Oh, my." Lady Juliet stared at the antique compass. Ben had thoroughly cleaned it, using surgical swabs to get at the tiny bits, then polished it till it shone. He waited for her to smile. She did not.

"I had one just like this as a girl." Removing the compass from its case, she studied it front and back like a jeweler, minus the loupe.

"I picked it up on impulse," Ben said. "Made by Dolland of London, I think the man said. The case has seen better days."

"It's mine."

"Yes, of course. Happy Christmas," he repeated.

"I mean, this is the one I carried everywhere as a girl. When I lost it, I was heartbroken." Turning it over, she showed him a faint etching. "See there? J.L., for Juliet Linton."

Ben didn't know how he'd missed it. What he'd taken for random scratches was, in the mid-morning sun, a child's wobbly but readable inscription.

"Father used to say I was born holding a map," she said. "He had a collection. Old ones and new ones. Some bound in books, some framed under glass. He would point at spots where the cartographer had drawn some fantastical beast and tell me, 'Here be dragons.' I said I wanted to sail there and see the dragons for myself." She smiled at the memory. "When I was a bit older, I planned my route to travel the world. First I'd fly to Ecuador. Then I'd sail to the Galapagos islands, Argentina, and Brazil. He was so pleased, he gave me his compass for Christmas. When I was careless and forgot it somewhere, I felt as if I'd forgot him."

Ben reached across the table and took her hand. Like the rest of her, it was large, strong, and feminine. It was warm, too, like her soft brown eyes.

"Thank you," she whispered. "Where on earth did you find it?"

"Howell's Nonesuch."

"Impossible. I went there once a week for ten years, hoping someone had nicked it, then sold it for cash."

"It's a long story. Let's get back on the road, and I'll tell you."

Chapter Six

They took a ferry across the River Tamar. The Austin Ten kept the wind off, so they chose not to disembark as they crossed. From inside the car, they could still enjoy the sights: blue sky, choppy water, and seals bobbing along beside the boat. Then they were on the road again, their trip slightly hampered by the lack of signs, many of which had been removed or obscured to foil future invaders.

"Is that Tavistock Road?" Lady Juliet asked, shaking open her map. "I know where we are, but only if you can assure me that is Tavistock Road."

Despite the odd hiccup, Ben was glad of her help, which successfully guided him to Stonehouse graveyard well before noon. Following the caretaker's directions, they located the lost-at-sea memorial which listed Jacky Smith among the dead.

"No grave but the sea," Lady Juliet read. "A sad inscription. But a poetic one, too." She placed some flowers they'd picked up along the way, then brought out her Brownie camera and took pictures.

"If one turns out well, I'll frame it for Letty. A keepsake for her nightstand. Now, step closer to the plaque, please. Mind the carnations."

Ben groaned. "Don't be ridiculous. You're the one who's improving her home. I'm sure she'd rather have a photo of you."

"Hush. I can't abide false modesty," Lady Juliet said. "Letty adores you. Now smile."

He did. After she'd taken a few extra snaps for safety, he insisted on putting her through the same treatment. He wanted a candid photo of her, though he wasn't sure where he would keep it. His housekeeper, Mrs. Cobblepot, was a former schoolteacher, and like all schoolteachers, was both all-knowing and all-seeing. But he'd clear that hurdle when he got the print.

Afterwards, they climbed back into the Austin and motored to the spot Lady Juliet had suggested they place the mermaid, Bovisands Beach. She'd been there once before, and remembered it as peaceful and meditative, but that had been in summer. Now deserted except for seabirds, it was barren, brown, and rocky. The wind swept along the shingle, battering them mercilessly. Ben kept one hand on his hat; Juliet tied a scarf over her cloche.

"I'm already frozen." Shivering, she reached into her pocket and pulled out the porcelain mermaid. "Letty asked me to place it where the tide would carry it away, or else drop it into the sea. I thought it would be easy. But the shingle will be softer close to the water, and my shoes are already sopping. Do you think if we put it here, the tide will take it?"

"Yes," Ben said, basing his answer on where the thickest deposits of seaweed and driftwood lay. "Mind you, I'm a fair bowler, or at least I was. I could chuck it into the water."

"Do you think that's entirely proper? Treating Letty's offering like a cricket ball?"

"There's a uniquely English question." He chuckled. "'It's all very well *proposing* to fling a miniature mermaid at Plymouth Sound. But is it done, old boy? Is it done?'"

"Take this," she said, pressing the mermaid into his hand, "before I tell you where else you can put it."

Ben passed her his hat. "Careful. Don't let the wind have it."

He was close enough to the tide to simply hurl it into the water. But with Lady Juliet watching, he couldn't resist showing off his run-up, bound, and coil, releasing the little figurine at the top of the arc. It disappeared into the surf. Probably it was destined to work its way into the shingle like a discarded shell. But perhaps it would drift into deeper, darker waters, where mermaids and dragons and resurrected sons live, hidden from human sight.

"Well done," Lady Juliet cried, clapping.

Not according to my knee, he thought, refusing to acknowledge the pain aloud. *I'll be leaning twice as hard on my cane tomorrow.*

It didn't matter. She mattered.

Pulling her close, he brushed his lips against hers. Not insistently but gently; an invitation, not a demand. Her lips were soft and perfect, just as he'd imagined. That kiss decided it. His body told him everything he needed to know about the depth of his feelings. The sound she made, the way she clung to him, told him everything he needed to know about hers.

Taking her face into his hands, he kissed her again, long and deep, like he never had to stop. In minutes they would have no choice but to return to the car and go back to Cornwall; she would spend Christmas Eve with her mother, Letty, Dinah, and her faux husband, while he spent his with Mrs. Cobblepot. He had no idea what the future held, but he'd formed a new opinion about Christmas, one he would keep for the rest of his life.

"Happy Christmas, Ben," she whispered.

"Happy Christmas, Juliet."

THE END

Dr. Bones and the Lost Love Letter

Chapter One

By 10 February 1940, the tiny Cornish village of Birdswing was in crisis. This crisis had nothing to do with Britain's recently implemented food rationing scheme, which limited each citizen's ability to purchase bacon, butter, and meat. It was no good going to pieces over the government's efforts to allocate food-stuffs and prevent the widespread hunger experienced during the Great War. As country folk, Birdswingers had certain advantages over city dwellers. They could supplement their store-bought items by fishing in Little Creek or buying a share in the Pig Club.

Nor did the village turmoil concern the war, which was progressing uneventfully. First Lord of the Admiralty, Winston Churchill, called it the "Bore" War; even that most patriotic of Englishmen, Chief Air Warden and Special Constable Clarence Gaston, had called it "phony" in a weak moment. There had been no battles, no ground taken, and thankfully, no casualties. Between Christmas and Epiphany, many of Birdswing's sons had received two days' leave, returning fit and flash in their uniforms. If sitting around in France awaiting their baptism of fire had injured their nerves, they'd hidden it well, dancing and romancing with gusto.

The crisis didn't even concern the unusually cold winter, despite its having reached "Bloody York" levels, according to some. The snow was piled high and the roads stayed frozen, but Birdswingers had adapted. The vagaries of weather could never keep a Cornishman down.

No, the village turmoil revolved around that supreme foible of all tight-knit communities, gossip. Specifically—there wasn't any.

Every first-year medical student knew that critical vitamin deficiencies gave rise to various maladies. Too little iron caused cold hands and feet; lack of calcium led to muscle cramps; a shortage of Vitamin C loosened teeth and softened bones. And as Dr. Benjamin Bones had discovered, a critical deficiency in gossip triggered various symptoms in his fellow villagers.

The butcher, Mr. Jeffers, had reacted by turning into a fabulist, handing out nuggets of ersatz information with every joint of beef. "By April, the King will arrive on Bodmin, mark my words," he'd blithely lied, passing a neatly-tied meat parcel across the counter. "London isn't safe for His Majesty, so he'll remove to the moors and live in a hut under an assumed name." When Ben asked the butcher why he'd begun trafficking in obvious deceit, he'd replied, "Stratagems, Doc. Spreading falsehoods is an old Cavalier trick. He who disputes the lie lets slip the truth."

This approach might have befuddled the Roundheads in 1649, but in 1940 it did nothing but make Mr. Jeffers less popular than his meat prices, which was saying something. Meanwhile, the proprietor of the Sheared Sheep, Angus Foss, renowned skinflint and celebrated crank, had begun arguing with anyone who looked at him crooked. He'd even gone so far as to alienate those cantankerous old time-wasters who made up his core clientele, accusing them of being, in his words, "cantankerous old timewasters." To punish them for loafing more than drinking, he'd hidden the pub darts (leaving the board up as a silent recrimination) and done away with the racy postcards behind the bar.

Ben's across-the-street neighbor, Mrs. Parry, suffered more than most during the gossip drought. She'd even lost weight, strengthening the perception she literally subsisted on rumors and innuendo. Lately Ben had glimpsed her walking the streets at various hours, looking about hopefully as if something scandalous might fall from the sky. Meanwhile, Ben's orange tabby cat, Humphrey, seemed too depressed to leave home. Instead of roaming the countryside, the tom now spent his days lying in a patch of sun, desultorily licking a paw.

Even one of Birdswing's most notorious figures, Ethan Bolivar, recently-reconciled husband of Lady Juliet, had failed to deliver. Dashing, charismatic, and deceitful, Ethan kicked off trouble wherever he went. But instead of settling in, Ethan had departed after the twelfth day of Christmas, going to Plymouth for what Juliet and her mother, Lady Victoria, called an extended business trip. As Ethan had no legitimate business, only a history of bad debts and felonious near-misses, the villagers assumed his trip was mere cover for more gambling and womanizing. Yet Juliet, who'd shocked everyone by taking him back, remained serenely silent on the topic. Reluctantly, Birdswingers had concluded that Juliet's earlier protestations had been pure theater, and a reunion with Ethan was all she'd ever wanted. This was understandable, given the gravity of their commitment, but he'd made a fool of her time and again. It was hard to watch their spirited, outspoken Juliet lie down like a doormat and invite Ethan to walk all over her.

If they only knew, thought Ben, smiling.

He was sitting behind his big black-lacquered desk, which dominated his office in Fenton House. The impressive desk, inherited from his predecessor, had five drawers. The bottom drawer on the right contained a King James Bible, one of the few things Ben knew Mrs. Cobblepot, his housekeeper, would not move or attempt to scour if she came across it during one of her daily cleaning raids. Inside the Bible, he'd tucked a snapshot of Juliet taken a few months ago, during their excursion to Plymouth. When he was alone in the office, he often took out the photo and studied it, wishing he could connect with the woman herself as easily.

In Birdswing, there was no such thing as privacy. Not the sort that he had known from birth as a native Londoner. In London, one was surrounded at any given moment by dozens of people consumed with many personal goals, not the least of which was ignoring virtually everyone they met. When it came to strangers, or even acquaintances, people found a reason to look elsewhere, to avoid the opportunity to say hello, and if threatened with conversation, to shake open a newspaper and hide. Thus, it was no feat of skulduggery for a man to carry on an affair in London. He need only take a double-decker to another borough, meet his amour at a hole-in-the-wall club, and escort her to a suitably nondescript hotel. But none of these things existed in Birdswing. Not double-deckers, hole-in-the-wall clubs, or hotels, nondescript or otherwise.

Can't imagine her going for such a thing, even if it were possible, Ben thought, smiling at the picture. She disliked it; he wouldn't have traded it for a fifty-pound note. Standing beside a memorial on a windy day, Juliet had forced a smile even as she kept her hat in place with one hand and pushed back some loose blonde curls with the other. The uncertainty in her gaze—the vulnerability of a woman who disliked posing for pictures— made her very pretty indeed. Heaven only knew how fast things would be progressing between them, if not for her faux marriage.

Juliet and Ethan's situation, boiled down to its bones, amounted to patriotism on her part and newfound heroism on his. Ethan was spying for Britain, gathering information on domestic Nazi sympathizers. As his cover relied on his ties to the Linton family, a spy handler from Whitehall had traveled all the way to Cornwall to ask Juliet to halt the almost-completed divorce process. Naturally, she'd agreed; what good Englishwoman wouldn't? But as a result, because of the Official Secrets Act, she was required to pretend she and Ethan were back together. She couldn't drop the charade until the war ended, or until it made her a widow.

In London, we could have dinner, go dancing, take in the pictures, thought Ben, whose imagination didn't stop there. But in Birdswing, even romance by telephone was dangerous, as the switchboard operator routinely eavesdropped on calls. Even an old-fashioned love letter carried risk, as the postmistress (who was also the switchboard operator) would surely remark on correspondence from Fenton House to Belsham Manor and back again. It was a shame, since by this point, Ben had enough pent-up energy to write a scorcher.

Something creaked overhead. Looking up at the ceiling, Ben smiled again. The Fenton House ghost, Lucy, had fallen silent of late. Probably because another female had taken over the attic—Juliet.

The attic scheme, which Ben and Juliet had hatched together, was working beautifully so far. One weekly trip by car from the Manor to the village proper wasn't enough to arouse suspicion, so after running her usual Monday errands, Juliet went to Fenton House, arriving around eleven o'clock while Ben was still seeing patients. Going up to the attic, she resumed sorting and boxing Lucy's personal effects. Her sudden death had left behind a jumble of items, many of which could be sold to benefit St. Mark's or given away to the poor. This charitable endeavor put Juliet nearby, allowing Ben to go upstairs between patients and steal a little alone-time. Of course, Mrs. Cobblepot frequently popped in, too, so it was hardly the equivalent of an anonymous London hotel. But it was better than nothing.

One last patient, Ben thought, glancing at his watch. Reluctantly, he tucked the photo of Juliet back into the Bible and put it away.

It had been a busy morning. This was typical; Saturdays were usually smooth sailing, but by Sunday afternoon the water turned choppy. Ben, now a regular churchgoer who received considerable praise for setting a good example (and deserved none of it, as he attended to see Juliet) could scarcely rise after the dismissal before someone said, "Doctor, I hope it's no bother, but may I have a word?"

This "word" often turned out to be a full-blown complaint, including signs and symptoms. By the time Ben completed the short walk from St. Mark's to Fenton House, Mr. Scow had described his halitosis; Miss Jones had hinted at a mortifying rash; and Mrs. Garrigan, the new mum, had whispered something about a "concern." As she was holding her newborn son at the time, Ben had assumed this had to do with the baby. Because Mrs. Garrigan tended to worry, and because she'd already had one brush with death, Ben told her to come first thing on Monday, a quarter hour before his opening time. As expected, she arrived even earlier, and he was there to open the door.

"Good morning," Ben said to Mrs. Garrigan as he peeked in at Charles, asleep within warm swaddling. "I can't imagine a more perfect baby. What's the trouble?"

"Oh, no, Doctor, it's nothing to do with our Charles," Mrs. Garrigan said. "He's good as gold. It's me."

"Not feeling dizzy again?" Eight weeks before the newborn's arrival, Mrs. Garrigan had been hospitalized for deep vein thrombosis, or DVT. She'd responded well to a new wonder drug called heparin, and might never be troubled by the condition again. Or a new clot might be forming in her thigh or lower leg even now, destined to obstruct blood flow at the worst possible moment and put her in an early grave. "Headaches? Heart racing?"

"None of that, thank goodness," Mrs. Garrigan said. "I'm a little tired, keeping up with the wee one's demands, but it's a joy, isn't it? The only bit I don't fancy is forever boiling bottles."

"Milk still irregular?"

"Yes, and he's so keen for the bottle now, I'm not sure he'd give it up, even if my milk was more regular." Mrs. Garrigan's gaze darted around the office, lighting only briefly on Ben. "But I must try, because it's better, isn't it? Helpful, they say, in more ways than one?"

"Of course. But you aren't the first new mother to turn to formula and you won't be the last," Ben said reassuringly. "I reviewed the literature before I gave you those samples. A study in 1929 showed no difference in development or weight gain in bottle-fed babies. Cow's milk or goat's milk can be dangerous. But scientifically developed formula—"

"I don't mean that," Mrs. Garrigan uncharacteristically cut across him. "Sorry, Doctor. I'm all aflutter. My Felix couldn't get Christmas leave, and he missed the birth, you know, so Monday next he's coming home for seven days. Seven whole days! He'll be dead handsome in uniform, and I've missed him ever so much, but...." Trailing off, she stared hopefully into Ben's eyes as if trying to bridge the gap telepathically.

"In church, you said something about a concern," Ben prompted, wondering if he'd overlooked an essential clue, as he had during her first medical crisis. "Are you quite certain you're not experiencing renewed symptoms?"

"No, I promise. Only with Felix coming home and Charles, who needs me every hour God sends...." She fell silent again.

"Is it your husband? Are you worried he won't know how to cope with the baby?"

"Gracious, no. He has five brothers and six sisters. I expect he'll teach me a trick or two."

"Then what?" He cast about in his mind for new mums' rarer complaints. "Are you afraid Felix will feel neglected? Jealous of the baby?"

Mrs. Garrigan shook her head. "Never. It isn't Felix. It's me. I—" Once again, words failed her, and she blew out her breath, defeated. "Oh, forgive me, Dr. Bones. There's nothing the matter. I should never have taken up your time."

With that, she'd fled. Ben had followed her all the way to the High Street, but she wouldn't return to his office or say anything more, except sorry.

After Mrs. Garrigan, he saw a farmer with an infected toenail and a crofter's wife with a nasty burn. Then came a little boy who'd taken to swallowing various objects to protest parental tyranny: bedtime, bathtime, veg before pudding, etc. The boy's mother, clearly at her wits' end, wanted Ben to lecture her child on the dangers of choking. After donning his starched white coat and head-strap mirror reflector, Ben had interviewed the boy. It seemed that after swallowing a tadpole over the summer, the child had received attention heretofore undreamt-of, inspiring him to perform more daring feats using buttons, pennies, and his sister's paper doll.

"I don't reckon I'll choke," the boy had told Ben. "I'm experienced."

"Clearly." Ben had sighed in the manner of a great healer forced to deliver grim news. "But when it comes to swallowing things, there can be unforeseen consequences. Tadpoles are very bad. Especially when followed by ice cream. It makes them multiply. Odds are, you've bred a colony of frogs. I'll bet you've felt them hopping around."

Eyes widening, the boy had nodded. Most children would agree with any statement made by a man in an impressive white coat with a shiny metal disc strapped to his forehead.

"You must prepare yourself," Ben had said dramatically. "The cure is rather extreme."

There he'd overplayed his hand. Little girls threatened with an operation tended to foresee fear, pain, and forced bedrest. But little boys often reveled in shocking proposals, going along boldly until words became action.

"Cut me open and pull them out!" the boy had urged him.

"Yes, well, I would," Ben had said, ignoring the mother's frantic throat-clearing. "Only your history of swallowing other objects renders surgery impossible. No, unfortunately, we'll have no choice but to starve them out. That means absolutely no pudding, cheese, milk, or candy. Nothing for you but water and bread crusts. Oh, and no wireless. Frogs have been known to rally and live twice as long in boys who listen to adventure stories."

That proposal got the desired response. Once the boy had vowed to stop swallowing objects if he could avoid such a draconian cure, Ben finished up by peering down the child's throat with a handheld torch and announcing that by some miracle, he saw no gastric amphibians clinging to the stomach lining.

"You're very lucky. But remember," he'd warned the boy, "from now on, you must swallow nothing but food and drink. If I hear differently from your mother or teacher, it'll be nothing but bread, water, and schoolbooks for six months."

After the tadpole-swallower, Ben had seen Mr. Jeffers. A red-faced, big-bellied man with a ginger mustache and a gap-toothed smile, he'd come in whistling, but made the same complaint as he'd made two weeks before: indigestion.

"It's always there, Doc," he'd said, buttoning his shirt up over his vest after Ben finished listening to his heart and lungs. "This must be how dragons feel, priming to belch fire. Bloody sprouts."

"As I said before," Ben had said, striving for patience, "however much you dislike rabbit food, as you call it, a spoonful of greenery doesn't trigger protracted indigestion."

"And now we have it," Mr. Jeffers had muttered. "'Cut down on beef. Cut down on starch. Take exercise. No fags, no pints, and no excitement.' Bloody Bolsheviks and vegetarians put about that rubbish to make us weak." He'd patted his midsection. "Doc Egan told me this lot pushes my choler into my windpipe. Hence my *choleric* nature," he'd said wisely. "So the real trouble is an imbalance of humors. That's what's wanted, for you to equalize my humors."

"I see." Ben hadn't taken offense. It wouldn't have been Monday if at least one patient hadn't lectured him on some medical theory, even one that had been abandoned around the Battle of Trafalgar.

"All this rot about twigs for breakfast and blades of grass for lunch is unscientific," Mr. Jeffers had said. "It's not that I wouldn't like to reduce. Last year, a pub stool collapsed when I sat on it. That wounded my pride, it did. But you can't fight nature. My old dad was stout, too."

"Remind me. What did your father die of?" Ben had asked, knowing the answer.

"Heart attack."

"How old was he?"

"Thirty-eight."

"Rather young. How old are you?"

"Thirty-eight." Mr. Jeffers's eyes had widened. "Come now, Doc, you can't draw a comparison. My old dad never cracked a smile. My mum died bringing me into this world, and I think part of him went out with her. A good man, mind you, but grim. His heart attack was brought on by overwork. The girl I walk out with says—" Mr. Jeffers had stopped there. "That is, the girl I used to walk out with, the one who fed me the bleeding sprouts, used to say I like a good time and that's my saving grace. Always one for a laugh, that's me. I may be the spit and image of my old dad, but I whistle while I work, and he ground his teeth."

"You're lucky to have a saving grace," Ben had said. "Not to mention a girl who cooks for you. Don't tell me you two went your separate ways over a dish of sprouts."

"She poisoned me." Mr. Jeffers had said unconvincingly.

Ben had folded his arms and waited.

"She knows my feelings on the green stuff, but she insisted. And what's the good of cooking a man a meal if you're going to harp on what he eats like he's a boy in short trousers? And for months she's been at me to...."

"To what?"

At that point, Mr. Jeffers had become interested in examining the tops of his shoes. "I suppose I do have something in common with my old dad. He swallowed his words along with his breath, as the saying goes. Don't get me wrong. I know I was dear to him. It was me and him against the world. But he never got round to saying so. Maybe he was waiting for the right moment. But one day we were mincing the silverside and he drew up short. Opened his mouth and stared at me like I was a stranger. Then the black swallowed the blue — in his eyes, I mean—and he fell on his face like a calf struck with a ball peen hammer."

"Thirty-eight," Ben had repeated. "It seems too young."

"As for Ernestine... it's not that I don't have something to say to her," Mr. Jeffers had continued as if Ben hadn't spoken. "One day I'll say it. But she pushes too hard. Do this, eat that, tell me this, promise me that. If I tell you something, Doc, will you promise not to laugh?"

"Of course."

"I know what she wants me to say. A man would have to be daft to miss the hints she's dropped. But I get a little speech ready, and it sticks in my craw. Next thing I know, I've got a cauldron in my belly and I'm up all night, belching fire. It wasn't swallowing the sprouts that gave me this indigestion. It was swallowing my own words."

"I can't laugh at that. As Englishmen go, it's practically an epidemic."

Mr. Jeffers's face had split into a boyish grin. "See, now, we understand one another."

"So take my advice. Spit those words out," Ben had said firmly. "Go round to Ernestine's, ask her to the pub, buy her a drink and *tell her*."

"But Doc, I told you, it burns right here," Mr. Jeffers had insisted, tapping the middle of his chest. "Isn't there a tonic or a salve you could give me first?"

"No, but there's a regimen. Cut down on beef, cut down on starch, take exercise—"

Mr. Jeffers's reply had been something he'd never say in front of Father Cotterill, much less a lady. They'd laughed, and he'd gone away saying, "Perhaps I will take your advice," in the reassuring tone of a patient who had no intention of doing any such thing.

Ben hadn't been surprised. He had a better chance of curing the common cold than of inducing the average man to voluntarily cut down on meat or starch. Perhaps the ration would accomplish what the scoldings of dietitians could not.

The special bell rang, jarring him back to the present moment. Rising, he went to answer the door, but his last patient had already let herself in.

Mrs. Richwine, Barking's oldest resident, was reputedly ninety. A widow of long-standing, she liked to dress in lavender from head to toe. In the nineteenth century, that shade had indicated "quarter-mourning." A quintessentially Victorian designation, it sought to express one's degree of bereavement mathematically, as a fraction of discontent. Those in mourning were also supposed to avoid personal embellishments, so Mrs. Richwine wore no jewelry apart from her gold wedding band and a tiny chip of jet in each ear. Ben, who like most men his age thought Victorian customs like lifelong mourning to be on par with medieval witch dunking, thought it was a strange choice for a woman as full of life as Mrs. Richwine. Despite the rumors, and the fact one never asked a lady her age, he estimated her to be no more than sixty-five.

A very short woman, she had a penchant for high heels and vertical hairstyles. Even so, the top of her towering white bun, secured with gleaming metal hairpins, barely came up to Ben's shoulder. "My dear Dr. Bones! How wonderful to see you again. If only it were under better circumstances."

"What sort of trouble is it?"

"At this time of year? On the very cusp of spring?" She chuckled. "What trouble can it possibly be, but heart?"

Chapter Two

"**Y**our heart?" Ben asked.

Her laugh sounded like the ringing of a crystal bell. "Oh, no, dear. My people are born sickly, but strengthen with age. I've never felt better. I mean the heart of a man whose letter went awry in the Fairy Post."

"I see," Ben said. After six months in Birdswing, he was losing his ability to be taken aback by curious statements. "Come through to my desk, please, and have a seat, won't you?"

She did so, looking around Ben's office, which was still decorated with late nineteenth-century relics inherited from Dr. Egan. "Well! Isn't this modern? Proves how long it's been since I've seen the inside of a physician's office. What's that?" She pointed at the phrenology bust. It depicted a surprised-looking man with his skull missing and various character traits like "Loyalty" and "Avarice" labeling sections of his exposed brain.

"Proof medical science can get it wrong," Ben said. "But what do you mean by 'Fairy Post?'"

"I'm surprised no one's told you," Mrs. Richwine said. "The Fairy Post has been in operation as long as I've been here, and I came ages back. But surely you've seen it. Before the snow fell, I used to watch you go rambling through Pate's Field, all the way to the boundary between Birdswing and Barking. Didn't you notice the hollow tree?"

"No. Wait. Yes, now I think of it. More of a tall stump, really."

"That's right. A storm tore off the crown and limbs. That was the autumn of 1916, when despair turned even the winds vengeful. But the Fairy Post has continued unabated," Mrs. Richwine said, "serving the lovelorn, the grieving, the hopeless, and the hopeful. Those last tend to be children, naturally."

Ben had steeled himself for nonsense, but this was exceeding his expectations. How long before he could shutter his office and go up to the attic? Trying not to sound as impatient as he felt, he said, "Forgive me, Mrs. Richwine. But I'd be lying if I said I understood where this is going, or what it has to do with me."

She issued that tinkling laugh again. "I do apologize. How is Lady Juliet?"

"I'm sorry?"

"Lady Juliet Linton. Well, Linton-Bolivar, I suppose. I'm devoted to Barking, having dwelt there so long, but the few times I've been privileged to have a word with Lady Juliet, her spirit has impressed me. I sense a worthy bloodline there."

For a moment, Ben felt as if Mrs. Richwine had read his mind. Then he remembered that Juliet's Crossley was parked outside Fenton House.

"Yes, well, by all accounts, Sir Thaddeus Linton was a remarkable man."

"Not him." Her eyes sparkled. "But never mind that. You asked about the Fairy Post. It isn't meant to replace the Royal Mail, but to work beside it, along the channels of magic and destiny. Children pen letters to Father Christmas, or Robinson Crusoe, or even a loved one they will never see again. Any destination they hope to reach that the Royal Mail does not serve. They drop their letter into the hollow tree and commend it into the hands of the fair folk."

"To be delivered into the pages of a storybook? Or the afterlife?"

"Who can say? The young possess such remarkable powers of hope," Mrs. Richwine said. "If such belief could be distilled into an elixir, a single golden spoonful would cure us all. Alas, that is not the way of things. So relatively few adults employ the Fairy Post. The destinations they intend aren't always impossible, strictly speaking, but they may be improbable, or ill-advised."

"Lonely hearts letters, you mean? How extraordinary." *Extraordinarily foolish*, Ben added privately, though he tried not to look surprised.

"Yes, or letters requesting help from the Shining Ones," Mrs. Richwine said happily. "That was the original function of the hollow tree: a repository for wishes and offerings. Few could write in the old days, so a learned man once sat under the tree, taking down petitions on scraps of paper. Into the tree they went, along with a coin or trinket for the Fairy Queen, whom the Romans called Diana."

"I suppose when no help came, the people blamed themselves instead of the scribe? Who must have lived rather well, I should think, if he emptied the tree each night." Ben spoke lightly, and Mrs. Richwine took no offense.

"Ah, but remember, the hollow tree was once a thing of beauty, with lofty boughs and masses of green leaves. The knothole for petitions and offerings was no bigger than my fist. Time and weather may have wounded it, but whatever is dropped into the trunk still disappears."

"Has anyone looked under the Archer twins' mattresses?"

She laughed. "I shan't pretend those boys haven't tried to interrupt the Fairy Post. But ask them how well they succeeded."

"Let me see if I understand. People drop letters into the tree," Ben said. "Some are delivered, some aren't. And no one is troubled by the idea that one of their neighbors is removing the letters, reading them over, and choosing which to distribute and which to burn? Or save for future blackmail, more like."

"For shame, Dr. Bones," said Mrs. Richwine, again with the tinkling laugh. "Your experience with murder in Cornwall has made you think the worst of us. The fair folk would never permit that, even if one of our friends and neighbors decided to commit such a sin against the community. The petitions for a healthy baby, or a bank loan, or a soldier to come back safe and sound, are whisked away to the other realm. The letters than cannot or should not be delivered in our world disappear to somewhere else. Once in a while, a letter comes through someone's post slot in the dead of night, or is found on their front step, tucked between the milk bottles. And once in a very great while, something goes wrong, and mortals must finish what the fair folk began."

Ben nodded vaguely, still wondering what all this bucolic superstition had to do with him.

"As I mentioned, spring is upon us," Mrs. Richmond said. "The vernal equinox won't arrive until the twenty-second of March, but the Green Man is already afoot. Just this morning I spied tender shoots, buds bursting, and hellebores poking through the snow. Soon the chiffchaffs will take wing! As I searched the trees for signs of life, what did I spy but this, stuck in a tangle of ivy."

Opening her bag, she withdrew a letter in a blank envelope. The seal, a bit of Sellotape, had been broken.

"I'm afraid I did have a look," she admitted. "By custom, letters deposited into the Fairy Post have no direction, nor any names, either in the salutation or the signature. What good is magic if such mundanities are required? At any rate, I thought if the letter was written by one of my fellow Barkers, I might recognize the penmanship. Alas, I did not. Therefore, the letter must have been written by a Birdswinger. That's why I've brought it to you."

"Me?" Ben stared at her. "I won't be able to guess who wrote it. I haven't lived here long enough to suss out villagers by handwriting alone."

"No, of course not," Mrs. Richwine said. "But in this case, it doesn't matter. The letter is dated 10 February 1913. Today's date, but for the year. Isn't that a marvelous coincidence?"

Ben had the uncomfortable suspicion it wasn't a coincidence at all. Did Mrs. Richwine's obvious passion for the Fairy Post signal that she was the anonymous force behind which letters were delivered, and which disappeared? Had she been collecting and reading them throughout her life?

Don't get carried away, he told himself. *Not many sweet little old ladies are capable of clambering into hollow trees, at least without being caught.*

"Take it," Mrs. Richwine said, passing the letter across his desk. "It's a love letter, and due to be delivered, either to the recipient or back to the author. Don't look so appalled, Dr. Bones. The Fairy Post goes awry from time to time, but it never fails. The fair folk dropped this into my path for good reason. And because you're one of Birdswing's most distinguished citizens, I'm dropping it into yours."

"Why not Lady Victoria? Or Lady Juliet?"

"Either would do an admirable job, I have no doubt," Mrs. Richwine said. "And you may consult them, of course, or anyone you wish. But you are a physician, and therefore best equipped to navigate uncertain waters. Particularly if the letter is destined to return to the writer rather than the recipient. A physician can address matters that gentlefolk, or even a man of the cloth, like Father Cotterill, cannot."

"If I accept this," Ben said, tapping the envelope in front of him, "I'll quite likely burn it. That strikes me as the wisest course. Not to mention kinder than reading someone's private business from thirty years ago and then showing it around the village, opening up old wounds."

He expected Mrs. Richwine, who had maintained unshakable sunniness throughout the interview, to take offense at last, snatch up the letter, and look for someone else to be her catspaw. It still seemed only logical that she'd nicked the letter ages ago and carried it into Birdswing simply to start trouble.

Once again, the little woman's eyes sparkled as if she read his thoughts and found them amusing. "My dear Dr. Bones, if upon reflection you choose to burn this letter, then that is the end the fair folk desire. They're very wise, you know, and rarely seek mortal aid except when they feel certain that mortal is up to the task. Like the Lady of the Lake bestowing Excalibur on the king," she continued, rising. "It wasn't every dark age chieftain who was so favored, but Arthur Pendragon, and from Dozmary Pool in Bodmin. He was chosen. Now, so are you."

* * *

Ben used his cane to climb Fenton House's steep stairs. Although he still resented the necessity of carrying it, winter had taught him a thing or two about post-traumatic arthritis, specifically of the knee. Pride was all very well, but it didn't cushion a man's arse when a joint froze up and he toppled over.

A cul-de-sac at the end of the upstairs landing contained four steps and a rather curious door. It seemed to have been reincarnated from a prior existence. For one thing, it was unusually thick, even after being cut down to fit the frame. For another, its deep linear scars suggested it had once been iron-banded, like the door of a cathedral or fortress.

The first time Ben encountered the door, it had been mysteriously jammed, prompting Juliet to open it by force. After that, it became prone to slamming, usually in the dead of night. Lately it had begun opening on its own.

Rather like a Venus flytrap, Ben thought, but without foreboding. He looked forward to these attic meetings too much to be put off by the eccentricities of an old door.

The broader footpath made walking with a cane easier. The attic landscape, though still chaotic, was improved: half-sorted heaps, a few sealed boxes, and a makeshift nook at the attic's far end, under the dormer window. And on a pouf beneath that window sat Juliet, nose in a book.

"Reading on the job?" Ben asked.

"Reading *is* the job. Fully half of it, at any rate, while I'm waiting for you," she retorted without looking at him. "What took so long?"

"Mrs. Richwine, from Barking."

Juliet's eyes flicked up. Like any naturally inquisitive person, she was curious about the lives of her fellow villagers, particularly when they visited Ben's office. But when it came to Barkers, for whom she generally maintained a true Birdswinger's antipathy, the desire to hear about their medical woes nearly overwhelmed her good manners. She knew Ben wouldn't discuss it, not with her or anyone else. Nevertheless, he heard the narrowly repressed curiosity in her voice as she murmured, "I do hope she's well."

"She is. Came to see me about some local tradition. But never mind. I have asked you not to wear that."

"It repels dust," she said, eyes back on the page.

"It repels more than that." Ben closed the gap between them, the better to frown over her usual attic uniform: a housedress, big as a mainsail, and a brown calico scarf tied over her hair. Propping his cane against a crate of bric-a-brac destined for the next church jumble, he said, "It's one thing to sort rubbish. Quite another to drape yourself in it."

She didn't look up. "If you dislike my appearance, Dr. Bones, I suggest looking away."

"Oh, so it's 'Dr. Bones' now, is it?" Taking the book from her hands, he untied the calico scarf and let it flutter away. "That's better. Now get rid of the sack."

"Hardly a sack." She slipped out of the housedress, revealing the trousers and the smart red twinset underneath. It was a simple ensemble, one Ben probably wouldn't have registered on another woman, but on Juliet it struck him as almost provocatively attractive. For one reason: it was worn by her.

"Why are you still on that pouf? Stand up."

"You're terribly dictatorial today. Suppose I resist?"

"Then I'll be charming."

She snorted. "You know my opinion of men with delusions of

69

charm." Instead of rising, she shifted onto her knees, reaching up to slide her arms around his neck. It made a nice change, her looking up at him for once. "You left the attic door open."

"It has a mind of its own. Maybe it's welcoming us inside. Or maybe it's trying to help Mrs. Cobblepot catch us out."

"I thought the same," Juliet said. "Maybe Lucy has taken against me."

"Why would she do that?" Smiling, Ben spooled one of her blonde curls around his finger and tugged gently. Dinah, Juliet's lady's maid, strove to send her mistress into the world with flawlessly arranged hair. Unfortunately for her efforts, Ben preferred it a touch messy.

"Maybe she thinks I'm not good enough for you. You and Lucy have some sort of channel between you. She comes to you in dreams."

"I'd rather it was you." He kissed her. Her lips were warm and soft, her skin fragrant with a scent that was hers alone, not from a bottle. Before long, his hands were drifting.

"Ben." Juliet's fingers closed over his, dragging his hands back up to her waist. "At least close the door."

"Bugger the door. Am I boring you?"

She answered with a kiss so passionate, it left them both breathless. "This is dangerous."

"No, it's not," Ben said, not fooling her and certainly not fooling himself. There was a reason people played with fire. Human beings had been doing it since the dawn of time, despite laws, statistics, and the occasional smoking ruin.

His lips found that magic spot beside her ear, the place where a kiss was as good as a key. Juliet made a soft sound, and just like that, his hands were free. When she pressed against him, that got the temperature up. Then he was kissing her with abandon, smoking ruins be damned.

"Dr. Bones!"

The attic stairs squeaked beneath Mrs. Cobblepot's heavy tread. Although sixtyish and generously proportioned, as she liked to put it, the housekeeper could move at a fair clip when she wanted. Mere seconds after she called Ben's name, her bulky shape filled the attic doorway. Juliet hurried forth to meet her; Ben turned his back.

The trick was to look innocently preoccupied. Seizing the church jumble box, he peered into it as if fascinated. Mrs. Cobblepot had retired from the classroom many years ago, but she retained the bloodhound nose and all-seeing eye of an experienced primary school teacher. Little things rarely escaped her notice; the obvious never did. Therefore, Ben couldn't allow her to see him until he was fit to be seen.

"Oh, my. You've made some lovely progress, Lady Juliet," Mrs. Cobblepot said doubtfully. Everything about the attic offended her. The dust, the dark corners, the metastasizing heaps and the swelling piles. Each time she entered the attic, her instincts cried out to attack. Ben knew she wanted to sweep, mop, scrub, wax, and finally bring out her ostrich feather duster on its telescoping pole and poke at the rafters till they knew who was boss.

"Thank you," Juliet said brightly. "I'm working as fast as I can, nose to the grindstone, no quarter asked and none given. I'll have this place shipshape and Bristol fashion before you know it."

Ben suppressed a sigh. Since she'd been drawn into Ethan's spy career and the unavoidable lies that went with it, Juliet had become better at dealing in falsehoods, but not by much. Typically, when she trotted out an untruth, she oversold it.

"Yes. Well." Mrs. Cobblepot indicated the pouf, stack of books, beat-up writing desk, and cracked vase full of dried flowers. "Tidy little reading nook you've made for yourself there, your ladyship. Looks a bit like you're settling in." She cleared her throat. "My offer to help still stands. I won't rush you, I promise."

Now she was the one overselling a lie. Clearly, it flummoxed Mrs. Cobblepot to see the usually swift, decisive-bordering-on-dictatorial Juliet Linton-Bolivar progressing at the speed of a Galapagos tortoise. And not just any Galapagos tortoise, but one who felt ambivalent about the whole endeavor and kept trundling back to the prickly pears.

"I'm ever so grateful," Juliet said, "but I feel a responsibility to handle each and every item with care. They all belonged to Lucy or her parents, after all, and I have good reason to believe Lucy is watching my progress. Besides, who knows what treasures I might uncover? Last week I found a pound note tucked in a bundle of household receipts. Perhaps I'll find a fortune if I go a little slower."

"Slower?" Mrs. Cobblepot sounded incredulous.

"And I wouldn't dream of shifting another burden onto your shoulders," Juliet added, shooting a glance at Ben as if trying to ascertain how much longer he needed. "Not when you're devoting so much of your spare time to the twins."

The twins were Caleb and Micah Archer, local scofflaws and budding anarchists. Recently, the boys had lost their father and very nearly lost their mother, prompting Mrs. Cobblepot and her brother, Chief Air Warden Gaston, to provide extra supervision whenever possible.

"Keeping the lads properly occupied benefits us all," Mrs. Cobblepot said modestly, looking pleased by the compliment. "Idle hands are the devil's workshop. They're in the back garden right now, you know. Assembling Dr. Bones's Anderson shelter at long last."

Nothing splashed ice water on Ben's ardor like hearing that Caleb and Micah were on his property armed with hammers, screwdrivers, and heaven knew what else. He spun around.

"You didn't lend them my toolbox, did you? Only think what they could do with my ripsaw. Or my pipe wrench. It weighs ten pounds."

Mrs. Cobblepot laughed. "I wasn't born yesterday, thank you very much, and neither was Clarence. He's out there ordering them about. Rest assured he took an inventory before starting and they won't nick a nail. But what's happened to your mouth, Dr. Bones?" She squinted. "Are you bleeding?"

"No, no," Juliet volunteered before Ben could stop her. "It's only my lipstick." Producing a handkerchief, she wiped his mouth, transferring a deep red smear from his lips to the white cotton weave. "He was teasing me about it, so to teach him a lesson, I swiped a bit on his face. Then we forgot about it. Yes! Wasn't that silly of us?"

Ben forced himself to say nothing. Juliet needed to let him tell his own lies. He'd been on the verge of claiming a spontaneous nosebleed, which was reasonably masculine, at least.

"It's very bad of you to tease Lady Juliet until she snaps," Mrs. Cobblepot said. "You shouldn't pester a lady about her beauty secrets. Suppose she takes it to heart? Then when poor Mr. Bolivar comes home, he finds a wife who—"

"What brings you up?" Ben interrupted.

"Oh. Well. I've put the kettle on, that's all. I only wanted to know which sandwiches you'd like. Cucumber or Marmite?"

"Forgive me for snapping." Ben smiled apologetically. "Isn't there any roast beef?"

"All gone, I'm afraid. We won't have meat again till Sunday."

"I can't bear another slimy cucumber. I vote Marmite," Juliet said.

"Marmite it is," Ben agreed. "Thank you, Mrs. Cobblepot. We'll be down directly."

He waited until he heard the stairs creak, then pulled Juliet close and raised his chin for another kiss. It ended all too soon.

"Don't," he murmured, as she pulled away.

"We really must go downstairs, before suspicions are aroused. And *don't* be vulgar."

"You enjoy tormenting me. And why not? Tonight you'll go to bed with Bertie Wooster or Jay Gatsby," he complained. "The best I'll do is if Humphrey curls up at my feet. If you compare the two of us, he enjoys the more fulfilling life."

"Envious of a tomcat?" She tutted. "How typically male. My heart breaks for you."

"Prove it."

"I shall. I'll lead you to a cup of revitalizing tea, a plate of nutritious sandwiches, and a quarter-hour of wholesome conversation.

Since your moral character appears to be waning." She laughed. "But you never told me what Mrs. Richwine wanted. A local custom, you said?"

"Some rubbish about a hollow tree in Pate's Field. The Fairy Post, she called it. Apparently, a letter from 1913 went missing. Now it's turned up and she wants me to deliver it."

"How exciting!"

"That's what excites you?"

She laughed again. "Safely exciting, I mean. Let's go down to tea and discuss it."

Chapter Three

"**W**ell," Juliet said, eyes warm with excitement. "Let's see it, then."

Ben's kitchen wasn't large enough for three people to comfortably sit down together, so they'd settled in the front room for tea.

"I haven't even read it yet," he reminded her, passing over the letter. "Maybe Mrs. Richwine was pulling my leg about its age. That envelope may have taken a little rain, but I don't believe it spent decades out-of-doors."

"It didn't," Mrs. Cobblepot said authoritatively.

"Oh. So you agree with me?" Ben asked her. "That Mrs. Richwine has been gathering letters from the hollow tree, delivering some and keeping the rest?"

"Ben!" Juliet cried. Although Mrs. Cobblepot looked equally dismayed, she only tutted.

"Dr. Bones, I realize Mrs. Richwine is from Barking. Nevertheless, she is a very dear lady."

"Yes. Best of the Barkers. No question." Juliet opened the envelope and withdrew two pages, deeply creased but in excellent condition. "Here's the date. 10 February 1913. I don't recognize the handwriting."

"Nor do I," Mrs. Cobblepot said. "As for its state of preservation, there's a perfectly logical explanation. It wasn't lost in Cornwall. It was lost in Elfhame."

Ben let out one of those harassed noises, somewhere between a groan and a sigh, that he often failed to suppress.

"Don't scoff," Mrs. Cobblepot replied. "Dozens of generations before us believed such things, and I for one won't toss their collective wisdom on the rubbish heap. My grandmother, a very wise woman, told me the hollow tree was originally native to Elfhame. During a mystical convergence, the worlds shifted. Some of our land was lost, but we gained the tree in its place. Any child can explain it. Each time the veil thins, a slice of the mortal plane vanishes into Elfhame and something from the other realm comes through. That's how Britain gained Avalon—and lost it again."

"It's how we got the Loch Ness monster, too, I suppose," Ben muttered. Picking up his half-eaten sandwich, he forced himself to take a bite, followed by a sip of vaguely dissatisfying tea. He didn't particularly care for Marmite, which was no substitute for roast beef, nor had he fully accepted tea without sugar.

"I've always wondered why the fairies put up with such business," Juliet said. Having already demolished one Marmite sandwich, she reached for another. "Losing part of their magical realm for part of our decidedly un-magical one, I mean."

"In the case of the hollow tree," Mrs. Cobblepot said, "they received an acre of barleycorn, or so the story goes. A small loss for us but a great gain for the fair folk, as they do not sow. However, they will reap, on occasion, if the result is liquor. And in Elfhame, a ripened field of good Cornish barleycorn never withers or depletes. That's why the letter has hardly aged. In Elfhame, the light restores and the air preserves.

"But getting back to the Fairy Post," she said. "I can assure you,

Dr. Bones, that Mrs. Richwine hasn't interfered with its operation, nor has any mortal. The tree is defended by magic."

"The sort of magic that can repel, say, Caleb and Micah Archer?"

Juliet laughed. "Yes, indeed. Last summer, Micah climbed into the hollow tree. On Caleb's urging, no doubt. I wasn't there to witness the attack, but Mr. Pate saw the aftermath. Dung beetles poured out of the tree's roots and attacked Micah like one of the Plagues of Egypt. He required special bath salts and two jars of ointment to recover."

"Are Cornish dung beetles dangerous?" Ben asked.

"Those are. Devil's Coach Horses, they're called. Like wee scorpions." Mrs. Cobblepot shuddered. "When I was a girl, they used to say don't muck about with the Fairy Post, or the fairies will muck about with you. After what befell Micah, a new generation believes it."

"It's a worthwhile part of childhood, I think," Juliet said. "I rather pity kiddies in London who grew up without it. There's something rather wonderful about dropping a letter into the dark and hoping with all your heart that the fairies deliver it. The last time I used the Fairy Post, I was fourteen. I sent a letter to Roald Amundsen. I knew I was too old for such nonsense, but it made me feel better."

"Who's Roald Amundsen? An unrequited love?" Ben asked.

"Hardly." Her tone was censorious. "Roald Amundsen was a noted explorer, as any educated person might be expected to know. First man to reach the South Pole, and first man to have reached both poles. I used to dream of accompanying him on a polar expedition. Intrepid girl explorer and all that."

"Why didn't you use the Royal Mail?"

"Because he was dead. Presumed dead, lost on a rescue expedition, never to return."

"And did you feel comforted after posting the letter?" Mrs. Cobblepot asked.

"I did. There's just something about taking one last stab. One final try, never mind the odds, before packing it in or crying uncle,"

Juliet said. "I find it easier to accept defeat, or to give up and grieve properly, if I know I've exhausted every avenue. That's why even adults turn to the Fairy Post from time to time, Dr. Bones. Not because we're softheaded in the West Country, nor even particularly softhearted. There's too much fight in us, and it dies hard."

"Why, Lady Juliet." Mrs. Cobblepot's teacup clattered against its saucer. "I'm surprised at you. A native Cornishwoman, discussing the Fairy Post as if it's some sort of psychological thingummy. As if magic doesn't exist at all. When only moments ago, you told us you were handling Lucy's things carefully, as you knew she might be watching."

Ben expected Juliet to take offense, or at least embark on a lengthy discourse about Dr. Carl Jung and the enduring relevance of psychological thingummies. To his surprise, she looked a little abashed and shot him a sidelong glance.

"You're quite right, Mrs. Cobblepot. Only... Dr. Bones *is* from London. Even after six months, I sometimes catch myself speaking to him as an outsider."

"I understand," Mrs. Cobblepot said. "But we're working on him night and day, and he's coming along beautifully, don't you think?"

Ben let out another harassed noise. Neither woman paid it the slightest mind.

"Well, now. Shall I read the letter?" Juliet asked.

"Yes, please," Mrs. Cobblepot said.

"Why not?" Ben asked sarcastically. "It's only some poor sod's personal business. I'm sure he'd enjoy having it read aloud to strangers over tea."

"Aloud? What a capital idea. I'd intended to read it silently." Juliet fluttered her lashes at him innocently. "Are we all agreed that the penmanship is masculine?"

"Firm and decisive," Mrs. Cobblepot agreed.

"What about bossy? Presumptuous?" Ben asked. "No? Fine. Not feminine."

Mrs. Cobblepot tutted again. Juliet regarded him through slitted eyes.

"There are some who would do well not to forget my powers of recollection, which are fearsome indeed." Clearing her throat, she read:

"'10 February 1913. Ah, Love. I never thought to write such a letter to you, or indeed to anyone. Once, I rejected the very idea of love letters. Like love poems, I found them artificial and altogether self-serving. Thus prejudiced against such a vehicle, I resolved that momentous declarations must be spoken straight out. In other words, simply and directly, rather than delivered in a literary concoction intended to wear down the reader through its cleverness, artistry, sophistication, and conceit....'"

"You wrote that," Ben accused her, only half-joking.

"He *is* an uncommonly erudite correspondent," Juliet agreed. "If one among us has hidden this flare for written language, I look forward to discovering who."

"Don't forget, people were a shade wordier in those days," Mrs. Cobblepot said. "More formal in their communications, too."

Juliet continued:

"'In our first meeting, you entered my life like a sea breeze into a windowless room that has known only stale air. Only then did I suddenly perceive the deeper mysteries those poets sought to illuminate.

"'From afar, I suppose the moment that changed my life must have appeared as prosaic as every other. The bell rang, as it does so many times each day, and I looked up, the welcome on my lips perfunctory and threadbare, divorced from all meaning....'" Juliet paused for breath before plunging on. "'And then our eyes met, and the worlds shifted. No poet would dare employ such a hackneyed phrase, yet I can think of no other. The insincere greeting died on my lips, as impurity cannot resist the cleansing fire; even an undeserving creature such as myself cannot persist in falsehood when faced with his ideal, his imago, his reason for living and, should fate demand it, his reason for relinquishing that life.'"

"We really shouldn't be listening to this poor man's rot," Ben broke in, chuckling uncomfortably. "Overwrought and ridiculous, wouldn't you—"

He stopped. Juliet and Mrs. Cobblepot were glaring at him as if he'd switched off the wireless during *It's That Man Again*.

"Rot, is it?" Juliet asked.

"Never mind him. Go on," Mrs. Cobblepot urged her. Juliet read:

"'Where once I believed any man with an hour and an ulterior motive could write intricate descriptions of his devotion, I find myself today with a free afternoon, a devotion so pure it astonishes me, and this uncharacteristic poverty of words.'"

Chuckling again, Ben felt the heat of the women's disapproval. He forced himself to finish his sandwich as Juliet continued,

"'Before I knew you, my existence was a foregone conclusion. I knew every step before I took it, every word before I said it, every choice before I made it. Loving you has swept away all certainty, bringing with it both fear and delight. My old life is dust and bereft of mourners, my old patterns of thought obliterated. I await each new day, each sunrise, with gratitude and an awareness of what can only be called grace.'"

Moving to the second page, Juliet said, "'Oh. This part must have been written rather hastily. Every other line is smeared or crossed out. It's dated 14 February." She read:

"'You will not accept my letter, will not speak to me, will not even look me in the eye....'" Frowning, she fell silent.

"What happened?" Mrs. Cobblepot sounded shocked.

"The affair ended," Juliet replied distractedly, still reading.

"That's it. As the only man in the room, I must speak up for this poor beggar, whoever he is," Ben said. "This wasn't meant for us to hear. We should burn the letter and be done with it."

"We've come too far for that," Mrs. Cobblepot said.

"Quite right." Juliet began again. "'14 February. You will not accept my letter, will not speak to me, will not even look me in the eye, after you uttered that last terrible speech.

"'You say it is over. That we must never see one another again. That I must forget what happened and disavow it utterly, as a madman, once cured, disavows his delusions. What am I to make of this?

"'Is what we shared so deplorable in your mind? Have you come to despise me, to find me morally repellant?

"'Rereading my own words now feels like an accusation. How ridiculous the page seems, exposing my grandiosity, my egotism writ large. Where were you in it, I wonder? I see only references to myself. What *I* believed. The possibilities which suddenly occurred to *me*. *My* transformation, the redemption of *my* character. Is that what drove you away? Did I forget to celebrate you, your charms, your virtues, even your foibles? I now comprehend what King Solomon meant when he wrote, "Then I looked on all the works that my hands had wrought, and on the labor that I had labored to do: and, behold, all was vanity and vexation of spirit, and there was no profit under the sun."

"'I realize you will perhaps never read this. Yet I have one final truth to tell.

"'When I was a boy, only one man in my village, Squire Philpott, possessed an automobile. It was an infernal thing, prone to failure. One day it surged out of control, struck a wall, and killed him. The steering apparatus collapsed and the exposed shaft pierced his chest. It impaled him through the lungs, not the heart, yet was a wound no man can survive.

"'I was there when Squire Philpott staggered free of the wreck. It was a sight I shall never forget. Not the blood or the gore but the look in his eyes, the terror and disbelief. He lurched about, keeping his feet for what seemed like an eternity, though it must have been only a minute. I think he was trying to behave as a man would after a lesser crash. To tut over the damage and hang the blame on some gear or cylinder. But all he could say was 'No, no, no.'

"'At last he dropped and was still. When I confessed to my father that I was relieved when Squire Philpott gave up the ghost, he replied, 'The poor devil was already dead.'

"'For years, I puzzled over my father's words. How can a man arise and move, however pathetically, and speak, however brokenly, and yet be dead?

"'Now I know. I comprehend it only too well, my love, my only love, my lost sweetheart. And it was no accident that I was one of the few people to behold Squire Philpott's sad demise. It was a foretelling of my own fate.'"

No one seemed to know what to say. After what felt like a long time, Juliet folded up the letter and slipped it back in the envelope.

"I wonder who wrote it. Not to mention who it was meant for."

"There's not much to go on," Ben said. Apparently, the habit of detection became increasingly difficult to resist, even in cases where it probably ought not be used. "We know the letter writer is male. We know he works in a shop, or once did. He's educated, clearly, though a prodigious vocabulary doesn't rule out self-education. Do either of you recognize the Squire Philpott story?"

Both women shook their heads.

"Then we know he was born somewhere other than Birdswing or Barking. That, and if he's still alive, he's probably around fifty years old."

"Angus Foss was born in Scotland," Juliet said. "He's fifty-two—no, fifty-three. But I can't imagine him writing such a letter. Then again, I'm not sure I've ever seen him write anything at all, apart from totaling receipts and marking his racing form."

Mrs. Cobblepot said nothing. She'd gone pale, as if the contents of the letter had touched her personally.

"What about your brother?" Ben asked her. "You two were born outside Birdswing, right?"

"Yes, we came as children. But Clarence never wrote that." Mrs. Cobblepot's voice quavered. "But I believe I know who did."

Chapter Four

Hole-and-corner, Juliet Linton-Bolivar thought on her way back to the village proper the next morning. As she had no bicycle, and petrol rationing meant she could only drive the Crossley once a week, she'd saddled up Epona for the occasion. An experienced equestrienne, she enjoyed the opportunity to ride, even if it meant she couldn't dress up for Ben. Besides, riding gave her the opportunity to collect her thoughts before she and Ben brought the lost love letter to their prime suspect.

Mrs. Cobblepot had convinced them that their quarry was none other than Birdswing's chemist, Mr. Dwerryhouse. He was the correct age, had grown up elsewhere, and like all the men of his profession, was extensively educated. Juliet had never heard of Mr. Dwerryhouse, who was unmarried, in any romantic context, nor had she ever stopped to wonder why. Yet the older residents of Birdswing like Mrs. Cobblepot knew a story about Mr. Dwerryhouse's failed youthful romance that they didn't repeat. And they didn't repeat it because it was hole-and-corner.

The phrase usually meant secret, albeit with an unsavory connotation, like black market beef or whatever business transactions the barmaid, Edith, conducted upstairs at the Sheared Sheep. But in Birdswing, hole-and-corner also had a special meaning, one that was, in itself, hole-and-corner. *That* was precisely the sort of circular peculiarity Juliet delighted in, now that she'd been clued in.

It had been a minor scandal concerning her lady's maid, Dinah, that opened the door. The previous autumn, Dinah had fallen pregnant and been abandoned by her still-unnamed lover. Terrified of the consequences, she'd concealed her condition to the end, giving birth in secret and leaving her newborn on the steps of St. Mark's. Often these situations led to tragedy, but thanks to Juliet, the baby boy had been adopted by a loving couple in Plymouth, giving both him and Dinah a second chance.

For weeks thereafter, Juliet had waited for the birds to sing. It wouldn't require Hercule Poirot to notice that the day after the foundling's rescue, Dinah had entered St. Barnabas's Hospital for undisclosed reasons. Or that she was listless and teary for weeks thereafter. Yet each week when Juliet had arrived at Vine's Emporium to look over the wares and catch up on gossip, no leading questions about Dinah had been asked.

"It's gone hole-and-corner, darling," her mother, Lady Victoria, had explained. "I can't take credit. Well, perhaps just a bit. Mrs. Parry stopped me after church to remark that Dinah seemed stricken, rather like a bitch whose pups were taken too soon. I'm afraid I looked down my nose at her, like the worst sort of snob, and said quite coolly, 'I do prefer it when the sermon touches on forgiveness and mercy rather than wickedness, don't you?' She fell over herself to agree, and that may have been the tipping point."

This had mystified Juliet, but upon further questioning, Victoria had insisted that Birdswing's essential nature remained unchanged. "The birds will sing when they will. I can't stop them, and neither can anyone else. Our collective sin as a village has always been a passion for gossip. But in some cases, the gossip is...." She'd paused, clearly at a loss to articulate something that apparently happened without discussion. "I don't mean to suggest we Birdswingers choose to ignore the more negative gossip. I'm afraid we enjoy bad behavior or a comeuppance far more than we should. But when the gossip has a pitiable quality, it triggers our collective decency, I suppose. In which case, the entire village goes mum."

"Just like that?" Juliet had asked.

"Just like that. Nicholas explained the phenomenon to me," Victoria had continued, referring to her late husband, Nicholas Linton. "He said once something's gone hole-and-corner, we never refer to it, except under extraordinary circumstances. He called it benevolent amnesia."

"That sounds like him." Despite her unshakable admiration for her late father, Juliet hadn't been sure she altogether approved.

"I'm pleased for Dinah, of course," she'd told Victoria. "But can it really be good, a group impulse to sweep things under the rug and ignore the lump, as it were?"

Victoria had smiled. "Probably not in every case. But a short memory can be a great virtue when it comes to village life. We can't always approve of one another, but refusing to dwell on disapproval is the next best thing."

When Juliet reached the High Street, she dismounted in front of Vine's Emporium. Fenton House no longer had a hitching post, but the general store had three, as Mr. Vine hadn't remodeled since the rise of the automobile. After reassuring Epona that the visit shouldn't take more than an hour, she fed the dappled white mare a handful of oats and started toward Fenton House.

The day was cold but bright. Was there a hint of spring in the air? Perhaps she was imagining it. Always a fresh air fiend, Juliet convinced herself every year that spring was coming early. This year it would be particularly welcome, as longer days would render the blackout less oppressive.

"Over here!" Ben called, waving to her from the patch of lawn between Fenton House and the neighboring cottage. As usual, he looked handsome in his black coat, red scarf, and fedora, which was cocked at a smart angle. "I'm inspecting my new shelter."

In the cottage's back garden, Juliet found an Anderson shelter as expertly constructed as the one on Chief Air Warden Gaston's own property. It didn't look terribly impressive, just a small shack with corrugated steel sides and a green roof bolstered with earth all around. But Gaston had made a study of its virtues, and between him and the informational programs on the wireless, Juliet had come to accept that if German bombs fell on their village, Ben and Mrs. Cobblepot would be safer inside the shelter than inside Fenton House. It was difficult to conceive of Birdswing as a Nazi target, but the whole point of the blackout was to confuse enemy bombers. Suppose in their quest to hit Truro or Plymouth, they struck Birdswing by mistake? She didn't like thinking about that any more than she liked contemplating a mustard gas attack. But one had only to revisit photojournalism from the Great War to picture those very things happening to her friends and loved ones.

"The twins did well," Ben said. "I made my own inventory of the tools and didn't find any missing. Think they've turned over a new leaf?"

Juliet laughed. "Civilization seems rocky enough these days without considering that sort of change. What's it like inside?"

"See for yourself," Ben said, smiling. "Come in and view my etchings."

She gave him what she hoped was a stern look. From time to time, he made what she considered a boundary-testing remark, most of which she pretended not to hear. Down deep, she enjoyed them, but it would never do to say so.

"It's even smaller than I imagined," she said, ducking her head to enter the shelter. "Thank goodness there's a bench. Otherwise I'd have to hunch over or sit on the floor. Which is damp," she added, taking a closer look. The shelter's single light bulb revealed an earthen floor that seemed to be taking in water at one corner.

"Gaston warned me that it may flood if we get the requisite April showers," Ben said. "He said I should floor it in. I could buy the boards from Mrs. Daley at the Co-op, but then I'd have to find time to do the job properly."

"It may be worth it. Imagine you and poor Mrs. Cobblepot out here all night in the cold, with coats over your pajamas and water rising over the tops of your shoes. Makes me grateful we have a wine cellar at Belsham Manor. We'll have room to move, we'll be too far away for Gaston to harass us unnecessarily, and I suppose we can uncork a bottle and pass it around if things get too grim."

"That sounds nice," Ben said, pulling her into his embrace. "Perhaps I'll get myself stranded there one night."

"You really must. Mother, Dinah, Bertha, Cook... they'd all be overjoyed to have you as company."

"Fair point." He kissed her, not the usual quick peck he gave her when they were in danger of discovery, but a long, luxurious kiss that took her out of the moment and into some personal Elfhame where they were finally alone.

"Ben," she whispered, resisting. "Someone must've seen us go in together. We need to leave. Now."

He sighed, unable to argue, and out they went.

"Have you thought of what you'll say?" Juliet asked Ben as they walked the short distance from Fenton House to Dwerryhouse's Chemist Shop. Its façade was sober, black and gold, and while many such establishments sought to exude an air of aggressive modernity, Dwerryhouse's looked as old as time.

"No." Ben frowned at her. "I assumed you would do all the talking."

"Me? Why?"

"Apart from the fact that you already do?" Ben grinned. "It just seems more natural for you to broach the subject of an unhappy love affair. Especially in this case."

"Oh, really? Why is that?"

He cleared his throat, a typical stalling technique. "You've known him all your life, for one thing. And you're a woman...."

"So I'm better suited to tackle something difficult, is that what you're saying? You're the physician. Haven't I heard you say there's nothing new under the sun, and you won't shy away from topics that benefit your patients?"

"Never mind that. Shouldn't you try and look at this from Mr. Dwerryhouse's point of view? What he might find easier?"

"You were charged with delivering the letter. You must be the one to present it. Never fear, I'll be there, silently providing moral support. Possibly with the occasional sympathetic nod of the head."

They'd arrived at Dwerryhouse's and its iconic window collection of bottles and flasks filled with liquids of red, sapphire blue, yellow, pale green, and pink. Since the rise of the pharmaceutical trade, a collection of such bottles had signaled "chemist shop" to the unlettered. The colors changed from time to time, as did the posted adverts and tableaus in the other windows, but that line of bottles and flasks never went away. They contained no drugs, performed no functions, and were much-mocked by the medical establishment, who considered them a perfect symbol for chemists in general: purveyors of potions that looked lovely and did nothing.

However, a glance at the patent medicine adverts made Dwerryhouse's seem like a nexus of fast, reliable healing. The signs proclaimed various offerings:

WHITE'S GOUT PILLS
  COOLEY'S TONIC BITTERS
  WEDGE'S COUGH MIXTURE
  WARNER'S TUSSO

as well as more general items inside:

TRUSSES
  ELASTIC STOCKINGS

CRUTCHES
ENEMA SYRINGES
NURSERY ITEMS
SICK-ROOM REQUISITES
ARTIFICIAL LIMBS ORDERED & FITTED UPON REQUEST

"I still think we're likely to humiliate ourselves," Ben said, hesitating by the door. "If Mrs. Cobblepot is so certain he's the author, why couldn't she recognize his penmanship?

"Penmanship can change over the years."

"I've never known Mr. Dwerryhouse to use so many grandiose words."

"It might be a habit he's abandoned, or one he reserves for the epistolary rather than the colloquial."

"Are you sure you didn't write it?"

"Mrs. Parry is watching from across the street. In!"

The twin bells above the door jingled as they entered. One of Mr. Dwerryhouse's assistants, Miss Miller, waved from behind the counter as the other, Miss Trewin, sailed up to greet them.

"Good afternoon, Dr. Bones, Lady Juliet. How may I serve?"

Miss Miller and Miss Trewin, neither a day over nineteen, always addressed customers in that fashion, whether that customer was an absolute stranger passing through Birdswing or a fellow villager they'd known from birth. They wore navy blue uniforms with starched white collars, kept their faces free of makeup, and pinned their hair up severely, like nurses.

"We'd like a word with Mr. Dwerryhouse. Is he free?" Ben asked.

"No, Doctor. He's in the dispensary." Miss Trewin indicated the pass-through window between the sales floor and the laboratory. "Would you care for a soft drink while you wait? We just got in a crate of Iron Brew from Falkirk. It might be our last."

Her caution wasn't merely a sales technique. Soft drinks relied on sugar and other ingredients that were rationed or due to be rationed. Soon beloved products like Iron Brew, Scotland's "second national drink" (after whiskey), might become scarce or disappear completely until war's end.

Ben glanced at Juliet to gauge her interest in a soft drink. It was a little courtesy she appreciated. When she and Ethan had walked out together, he'd ordered everything for her—cocktails, entrees, desserts —in a knowing tone that suggested he understood her desires better than she did. It wasn't that Ben never took control; she couldn't imagine bothering with a man who didn't want his hands on the wheel at least half the time. It was that Ben's ego was healthy enough to sustain itself without requiring him to dictate where others would clearly prefer to choose for themselves. Smiling, she shook her head.

"No, thank you," Ben told Miss Trewin. "We'll have a look at what's on offer."

As he studied a rack of proprietary elixirs, Juliet drifted over to Mr. Dwerryhouse's consulting room. It was the heart of his operation, a little office where his customers might feel at home. Its desk bore a leather blotter, brass lamp, and two of the chemist's best-known accoutrements, the mortar and pestle and the scale. Behind the desk hung his diploma from the Royal Pharmaceutical Society, received in 1909. On his sign and letterhead, he always went by A. C. Dwerry-house; only the diploma revealed his given name, Augustus Caesar Dwerryhouse.

Six days a week, Mr. Dwerryhouse consulted with villagers, answered questions, suggested remedies, and empathized when he could do nothing else. Juliet saw nothing wrong with this, and was glad Ben didn't, either. She knew that many physicians considered pharmaceutical chemists, or "pharmacists," like Mr. Dwerryhouse to be one step up from medicine show mountebanks. Fully half their stock was known to be useless, and once in a while, something was discovered to be harmful. Moreover, some physicians believed that the chemist's habit of offering free advice not only undercut doctors (who always charged to prevent the devaluing of their profession), but drove a wedge between the physician and his community. How could a doctor properly serve patients when they saw him only as a last resort, after attempting folk remedies that made the original problem worse?

But after a rocky start, Juliet had watched Ben and Mr. Dwerryhouse settle into a cordial working relationship. Mr. Dwerryhouse had clearly come to respect Ben's acumen, and she knew Ben had gained an appreciation of the chemist's role in the community.

Mr. Dwerryhouse's weekly infant weigh-ins, for example, were a public service. He kept detailed records, recommending supplements or raising the alarm if necessary. His willingness to cluck over children's skinned knees, hangnails, and stomach aches saved Ben time and the children's mothers, money. He used his medical dictionary to translate Ben's prescriptions, written by custom in abbreviated Latin, for anxious patients. After Mr. Dwerryhouse patiently explained the distinction between a scruple and a grain, or the difference between *alt. dieb.* and *alt. hor.*, even the most suspicious crofter might agree to purchase something as mysterious as sulfa tablets.

The shop door's bell rang. Reminded of the letter, Juliet turned to see Mrs. Garrigan enter. Since the new mother's hospitalization, they'd become friendly.

"Mrs. Garrigan," Juliet said, smiling to see the bundle in the other woman's arms. "And young master Charles. May I have a peek?"

"Why, yes," Mrs. Garrigan said. She sounded a wee bit off her game, but she obligingly pulled back the baby's blanket to reveal his sleeping face. "My beautiful boy. Would you like to hold him?"

As someone with no younger siblings, nor any history of child-minding, Juliet shook her head. "I wouldn't want to get it wrong."

"Cor, there's nothing to get wrong," Mrs. Garrigan said, pushing the baby into Juliet's arms before she could think up a graceful evasion that didn't involve running away. Jolted by the transition, Charles opened his eyes, saw Juliet, and immediately began to cry.

"Oh, er—" She tried to sort of playfully jostle him, as she'd observed so many women do with ease, and Mrs. Garrigan squeaked in alarm.

"Not like that, your ladyship, not like that," she said, taking her son back. In a calmer tone, she added, "It's all right to rock them, but you must support their head when you do it, like this. The wee ones aren't made of bone china, as I used to imagine, but they aren't granite, either."

Juliet looked about cautiously. As she feared, Ben was watching with obvious amusement. Miss Trewin, who'd been waiting for the right moment, said,

"Good afternoon, Mrs. Garrigan. Back so soon?"

"Oh. Well." She fussed with Charles's blankets. "I thought I might pop in out of the cold. Check his weight."

"But we checked it this morning," Miss Trewin said brightly. "I logged it in the book for Mr. Dwerryhouse, remember?"

"Oh. Yes. What a goose I am," Mrs. Garrigan said, still fussing unnecessarily with the blankets.

"Good day," Ben said, smiling in a way Juliet took down mentally for future vengeance. "I do hope you'll allow Lady Juliet to hold the baby again. That was a remarkable technique she demonstrated, which I'd like to study more closely."

"That's unkind, Dr. Bones. You'll give Lady Juliet the idea she's not cut out for motherhood," Miss Trewin said lightly.

"On the contrary, his insinuations on the topic affect me not one whit," Juliet said. She'd always found Miss Trewin prone to inserting herself into conversations without invitation. "Perhaps you should make certain you can't serve Mrs. Garrigan in some way?"

"Never mind," Mrs. Garrigan said, still rather squeakily. "I don't need anything. I'd forgotten Charles already had his weigh-in. Goodbye, Lady Juliet. Goodbye, Dr. Bones." Turning, Mrs. Garrigan hurried out of the shop.

Miss Trewin shrugged. "I don't envy new mums. Sometimes I think the experience turns them dozy."

"Yes, well, no doubt you're right," Juliet said. "Of course, in your case, when that happy day arrives, none of us will see any difference."

Miss Trewin's eyes widened. She possessed just enough good sense to work out that she'd been insulted, yet insufficient wisdom to withdraw from the battlefield. "That day will come for you first, I'm sure. If Mr. Bolivar ever makes Birdswing his permanent residence, of course. Perhaps all of us must work harder to make him feel welcome, hmm?"

"Hello, hello," Mr. Dwerryhouse interrupted in his usual friendly style. "Miss Trewin, there's a bit of filing to be done in the dispensary. Would you see to it, please?"

"Yes, Mr. Dwerryhouse," she said, and obeyed, but not without a defiant little toss of her head.

Taking a deep breath, Juliet silently counted to ten. One of the worst things about her faux marriage was the lingering implication in some quarters, generally female, that Ethan was the injured party, and Juliet to blame for all their troubles. It was yet another reason she and Ben had to take care not to be discovered. Men, especially unmarried men, were expected to indulge in a little mischief, be it drinking, gambling, or romance. But as the community's physician, no one would look kindly on Ben carrying on with a married woman. As for her—well, best not to imagine the consequences.

"I do apologize for keeping you waiting," Mr. Dwerryhouse said. A small man with a hooked nose, black hair shot with gray, and one shoulder a few inches higher than the other, he might've resembled a cinema henchman, but for his courtly manner. Those who complained that gentlemanly comportment had disappeared from the face of the earth around 1920 (specifically with the arrival of that American invention, jazz) had never met Mr. Dwerryhouse.

"I confess," he continued, "when I see the pair of you together I immediately think something mysterious must've transpired. Is this an investigation? Heaven knows the birds could use some fresh sheet music."

"Not an investigation, precisely," Ben said. "More of a curiosity. May we speak in your office?"

The chemist's small brown eyes lit up behind his equally small round specs. "Oh, my. Why, yes. Yes, of course. Come through."

Once they were settled in his consulting room, with Mr. Dwerryhouse behind the desk and Ben and Juliet sitting across from him, he said, "Now. What can I help you with?"

Ben, who remanded silent, shamelessly looked at Juliet as if she'd agreed to drive the conversation. He wasn't getting away with that. She stared back at him mutely, as if completely in the dark.

"Well. This is rather unusual," Ben said, clearing his throat unnecessarily. "It pertains to the Fairy Post."

Mr. Dwerryhouse didn't hide his astonishment. "Has another child climbed inside? You'd think they'd learn. If it isn't dung beetles, it's carpenter bees. Muck about with the Fairy Post and the fairies will muck about with you."

"So you, er, approve of the custom?" Ben asked.

The chemist laughed. "You seem at some pains to avoid asking me if I believe in it. And if you'd asked me when I arrived here, newly-qualified and steeped in academe, I would've said no. I grew up in Wiltshire, which has its own peculiarities and, I daresay, superstitions, but nothing like what one encounters here. Having said that, I've resided in Birdswing long enough to witness things that can't be explained away by misunderstanding or coincidence. So yes, it's fair to say I approve of the custom. I don't understand the Fairy Post, but I know that letters dropped into it seem to disappear, and I know that a few of them have been delivered."

"In those cases when they were delivered," Juliet said, deciding to help Ben just a little, "would you say the results were for good, or for ill?"

"Oh, for good, without a doubt. Any lifelong Birdswinger or Barker will tell you that when a letter is delivered, feuds are ended or broken friendships are renewed. It's always considered a blessing to receive a letter by Fairy Post."

Having been given such an opening, Ben couldn't fail to produce the letter and explain the task Mrs. Richwine had given him, which he did in short order. Mr. Dwerryhouse seemed intrigued.

"The letter's reappearance after such a long time is curious indeed," he said. "May I see it? You may depend upon my discretion."

Ben passed it over.

Mr. Dwerryhouse scanned the first page, read part of the second, and sucked in his breath. Shaking his head, he folded up the letter, popped it back in its envelope, and pushed it toward Ben like a magician making something nasty go *poof*.

"That has nothing to do with me," he said. "Who else have you asked?"

"Only you," Ben said. "There was some—that is to say—"

Clearly, he wanted to explain that Mrs. Cobblepot had steered them in Mr. Dwerryhouse's direction without using her name. Taking pity on Ben a second time, Juliet said, "You share certain qualities with the author. Age, presumed education, a childhood outside Birdswing. And it's been mentioned that years ago, you had a love affair that ended unhappily."

"That's a lie," Mr. Dwerryhouse said.

Juliet gaped at him. "I—well—only—"

Mr. Dwerryhouse stood up. "I find this all most irregular and disrespectful, yes, disrespectful of my position in this community. Forgive me for speaking bluntly, Lady Juliet, but this interview strikes me as a cruel prank. Mr. Jeffers has been spreading outright falsehoods for some time. Perhaps he concocted this letter in hopes of digging into my private business. I'm disappointed, frankly, that you would participate in this mischief, Lady Juliet, and shocked that you of all people, Dr. Bones, would go along with it. On the pretext of the Fairy Post, no less."

With that, Mr. Dwerryhouse exited the consulting room, leaving Juliet and Ben to stare at one another in mute astonishment. Juliet hoped the chemist would collect himself and return with an explanation. But it was Miss Trewin who came to consulting room, looking almost in tears.

"I'm afraid we're closed for the day. I'll see you out."

* * *

"How did it go?" Mrs. Cobblepot called when Juliet and Ben entered Fenton House.

Ben, peeling off his scarf and coat, either didn't hear or was too disgusted to respond, so Juliet said, "Not quite as we'd hoped."

Mrs. Cobblepot emerged from the kitchen with a beaded brow and raw, red hands. Even on a chilly winter's day, woman's work often entailed breaking a sweat.

"Did he admit to writing the letter?"

"No," Juliet said. "He demanded to know why we brought it to him. Rather than use your name, I said people knew of his unhappy love affair...."

Mrs. Cobblepot winced.

"Prompting a man I'd describe as unfailingly correct to call Lady Juliet a liar straight to her face," Ben said, dropping into a wingback. "He seems to think she and I were digging into his past with no aim but to humiliate him. Not that I blame him," he added, shaking his head. "Didn't I tell you that letter wanted burning?"

"A liar," Mrs. Cobblepot whispered. "Oh, my dear, I'm terribly sorry. I was certain Aggie wrote that letter to Bertie."

"Quite possibly he did," Ben said. "If he did, he wants the whole thing buried, and I can't blame him. Perhaps the story was never true, and that's why he reacted so strongly."

"It *was* true," Mrs. Cobblepot said. "It was so long ago, but I remember it well. Aggie walked out with me from time to time, only as friends, mind you, in the days before I met my Tom. I always knew Aggie would be a confirmed bachelor, even if he never said so, and of course he couldn't. Then he hired Bertie as his first shop assistant, and Bertie was irresistible. Shallow, bone idle, and nice-looking, of course, as so often happens. Even in his youth, Aggie was closed off. Unfailingly correct, as Dr. Bones put it. But he positively lit up when Bertie entered the room. It was—"

"It was no one else's business then, and it's no one else's business now," Ben cut across her. "This is turning into the worst sort of gossip. Mr. Dwerryhouse is the closest thing to a colleague I have in this village. I need to see him every day and work with him as smoothly as possible. I wish you'd never told me any of this."

Juliet was more shaken by Ben's tone then she had been when Mr. Dwerryhouse called her a liar. Mrs. Cobblepot looked stricken.

"I do hope this hasn't made you view Aggie—Mr. Dwerryhouse— differently," she said.

"It has. It's made me view him as a man with something to fear, who now thinks the village has resurrected a story that could cost him his livelihood and perhaps even his freedom. Worse," he told Juliet, "he thinks you and I came to confront him. That we handed him proof in the hopes of eliciting a confession."

"Oh, come now," Juliet said. "You're taking this too much to heart, just as he did. I suppose you assume because this isn't London, the small-minded denizens of the West Country will take up torches and pitchforks to drive him from our midst. I will remind you, I placed the complete works of Oscar Wilde in the Birdswing lending library and received no complaints."

Ben looked as though he wanted to laugh. Infuriated, she added, "Next you'll say it doesn't matter, because few if any of us can read!"

He sighed. "Don't let's argue. It doesn't do any good, what's done is done. Forgive me, Mrs. Cobblepot, for snapping at you. I've no doubt you meant well."

"I did." She sounded sad. "Bit of a guilty conscience, I suppose. Years ago, when Bertie went round making his accusations, I should've come to Aggie's defense, but I didn't. I didn't want anyone to think less of me for taking his part. And after Bertie had gone— paid off by Aggie, I shouldn't wonder—and things settled down, I kept my distance. I always thought I'd make it up with him eventually, once enough time had passed. But then I met Tom, and married him, and went away for years. Now he calls me Mrs. Cobblepot, and I call him Mr. Dwerryhouse, and it's as if we were never friends at all. I thought perhaps the letter surfaced because it was time for me to say sorry."

"You can still say it," Ben said. He no longer sounded cross, which didn't surprise Juliet. He never stayed angry for long. She had to struggle to rid herself of grudges and grievances, whereas he shifted easily from emotion into analysis.

Rising, Ben crossed the room to her, giving her a half smile. "And no, I wasn't going to suggest that no one in Birdswing has ever read *The Picture of Dorian Gray*. I was going to say that our library at university had every sort of book, from Oscar Wilde all the way back to Plato. It didn't stop the Dean from drumming out a student in my year for a similar accusation. He was talented. Top marks in Organic Chemistry. It didn't matter. Rather than endure being sent down in disgrace, he hung himself in the dorm while the rest of us were at dinner."

Juliet's lingering annoyance evaporated. "How dreadful. Was he —was it even true?"

"I have no idea," Ben said. "Once the word got out, I kept my distance from him, just like everyone else." He sighed. "We'll sort this out with Mr. Dwerryhouse somehow. We can't let him go for days believing the story is making the rounds again. But first, I'm taking this letter to the butcher shop. If Mr. Jeffers faked it in hopes of stirring up trouble, I want to know."

"I'm coming with you," Juliet said.

"No," Ben said, but gently. "I'd like you to stay here, in case Mr. Dwerryhouse turns up to mend the breach. I'll deal with Mr. Jeffers."

Chapter Five

Mr. Jeffers was not at the butcher shop. His assistant, a rail-thin, spotty-faced boy with an Adam's apple the size of a horse chestnut, stood behind the counter. Alone with customers for what must have been the first time, he looked frankly terrified when the bell above the door signaled Ben's entry.

"Mr. Jeffers wasn't feeling well," the boy said. "Went home to Owl Cottage. Had some bad sprouts, you see. Hasn't been the same since."

The bell's ringing followed Ben as he drove to Owl Cottage at the top of Mallow Street, where most of the ice and snow had thankfully melted away. Now that his irritation over the botched visit to Dwerryhouse's Chemist Shop had faded, he'd begun to doubt whether Mr. Jeffers could have devised such a complex bit of fakery. Not only did the butcher possess no special facility for language, but he didn't appear any more comfortable with emotional declarations issued on paper than he was at speaking them aloud. Had he been, he would surely have sent a written marriage proposal to Ernestine.

What about his father? Ben wondered. *If he'd lived, he'd be about the right age.* Perhaps the late Mr. Jeffers had written it to a woman who'd broken his heart so completely, he'd never spoken of love again, even to his only son.

There was still a bit of ice on the path to Mr. Jeffers's front door. Here, the cane Ben so resented proved essential, as the extra bit of leverage saved him from a nasty fall. The front garden was in disarray, which wasn't surprising. Mr. Jeffers practically lived at the butcher shop, and came home only to sleep. His front door needed a coat of paint, and the brass knocker was tarnished. Ben knocked.

No answer. Ben knocked again, louder, glancing up and down the street as he waited. The butcher's lorry was parked by the curb. That proved Mr. Jeffers had indeed driven it home, and not to the Sheared Sheep, which was his second most likely destination.

Still no answer. Going around to the back, Ben knocked louder.

"Come in," someone called softly. Ben couldn't tell if it was a man or a woman. The back door, like most doors in Birdswing, turned out to be unlocked, so he let himself in.

"Mr. Jeffers? It's me, Ben Bones."

"In here," someone called weakly. Ben followed the voice upstairs and into the master bedroom. There he found Mr. Jeffers sitting up in bed, supported by a pile of pillows. His face was gray, his eyes wide and frightened.

"Feels like there's a brindled cow on my chest," he said. "I reckon I'm dying."

"No, you're not," Ben replied automatically, in the abrupt tone he always used on frightened men. Too much sympathy would only deepen their alarm, which could be fatal. "Take slow, deep breaths. Only let me fetch my bag from my car and I'll be back to take care of you."

* * *

"I don't understand," Miss Ernestine Trewin, elder sister of the chemist shop assistant, told Ben. But from the look in her eyes and the flatness of her voice, he knew she understood perfectly.

"I can arrange for a sister from St. Barnabas to look after him for the first week or so," Ben said. They were sitting in Mr. Jeffers's kitchen, where they could speak softly without being overheard by the patient upstairs. Ernestine had put the kettle on automatically, but forgot to turn on the cooker, and Ben, not wanting to fluster her further, had decided to pretend tea was never offered.

"In the meantime," Ben said, "if you're willing to nurse him, I'm sure Mr. Jeffers will be grateful. No training is required. You need only keep his bedroom curtains drawn, keep the room quiet, speak to him in a low voice, and give him a little broth or weak tea if he asks. Should he try to get up, remind him that my strict orders are to stay in bed and keep still. This means a bedpan and sponge baths. No walking of any kind, for any distance."

He'd said all this before, twice in fact, and he knew Ernestine had already incorporated the instructions into her being. Thin and plain-faced, she carried herself with the air of a young woman accustomed to doing things, and doing them right.

"I'm sorry, Doctor. I understand how I'm meant to help Abraham. But I don't understand what *you're* doing to help him."

"I'm not doing anything," Ben said gently. "There's no treatment for a heart attack. Nothing but rest, and quiet, and prayers, if you wish."

"But you told him he wasn't going to die," Ernestine said. "I heard you tell him quite clearly that he wasn't going to die. But no sooner did we step into this kitchen then you told me he could go at any moment."

Ben nodded. "I know. I dislike concealing the truth from patients. But I was taught that it's often best, because many of them take the word of a physician as one rung below the word of God. To tell Mr. Jeffers this is the critical time, that he'll either survive the damage to his heart muscle or it will fail altogether, may take away his hope, and if I do that, it could be as good as killing him."

"But killing my hope makes no difference," Ernestine said bitterly. Digging in her purse, she took out a gold-toned case and withdrew a cigarette. Automatically producing his lighter, Ben lit it for her, shaking his head when she offered him the case.

"Why hasn't that bloody kettle whistled? Oh." She rose to turn on the cooker, then stood beside it for a while, back turned to Ben, smoking. Halfway through the fag, she whirled around as if remembering something important.

"Nora Garrigan! She lives on my street. She told everyone you saved her life by giving her a drug called hep—hep—"

"Heparin," Ben supplied.

"Why can't you give it to Abraham?"

"Because that isn't what it's for."

"You don't want to help," Ernestine accused, stabbing at the air with her cigarette. "Small wonder Nora can't ask you for Rendell's or French letters. She probably thinks you'll tell her to go away and never come back."

Ben blinked at Ernestine. "So that's what she wanted. She couldn't tell me. I even saw her in the chemist shop, but she couldn't tell your sister, either. You'd think her husband would take care of those matters."

Ernestine scoffed at that. "Yes, well, you'd think the Germans would keep to their own bloody patch and the King would sell off the crown jewels before taxing the working class. As for Felix Garrigan, he's a sweet lad, but he has the brains of a moldy potato. If Nora were nursing it might protect her. But as it stands, if she doesn't do something, she'll have another baby before the year ends."

Ben took that in. Ernestine, perhaps regretting her outburst, seemed relieved by the kettle's soft whistle. Stubbing out her cigarette, she busied herself with the tea, hands working deftly despite her clear unease. It confirmed Ben's suspicion she would make a good nurse.

"I hope you'll forgive me, Doctor. I shouldn't have spoken to you that way," she said, pouring them each a cup. "Of course Nora is afraid to speak to you. That's the trouble with this village. We live to gossip about each other, but we won't say what begs to be said. I've been hinting for Abraham to ask me to marry him. It's anyone's guess how that turned into a row over sprouts. I wonder if the row caused this."

"I can promise you it didn't," Ben said. "He himself told me all the things he ought to do for a longer, healthier life. And that his father died young."

"Yes, well, old Mr. Jeffers was a study in misery. I think he believed the world had passed him by. Wouldn't talk about the war. Wouldn't talk about much of anything, and couldn't read or write, apart from his own name. Mum says he was waiting for life to become simple again. When it didn't, he gave up." Ernestine set down her teacup with a clatter. "But Abraham has so much to live for. He's spent years building up the business to a modern operation. I even helped him with the books, and clearing up some delivery problems. I'm so cross with him, I want to scream! Suppose he dies alone in this house, with only a sister to care, because he wouldn't ask the bloody question?"

"What's stopping you?" Ben asked quietly.

Ernestine stared at him. "What's stopping me from what?"

"Asking him the bloody question."

"Dr. Bones," she said, shocked. "I'm not that kind of girl. Bad enough to be pushy and insinuating, which I've become, thanks to him. I could never... What would people say? Only suppose the story got out. What would people say?"

Ben was tempted to ask her if it mattered. But when it came to pushiness, insinuation, and outright interference, he felt guilty of all three. It was time to right the ship. Ignoring the question, he sipped his tea, waited a short interval, and asked, "Shall we go up and tell Mr. Jeffers you'll be staying for the next day or so to see to his needs?"

* * *

Ben had hoped to find Juliet waiting for him at Fenton House. Although it was past four o'clock in the afternoon, there was still at least an hour's daylight before the blackout took hold, and Epona could get her home, even in the dark. But Epona was no longer tied up in front of Vine's, and Mrs. Cobblepot was out, too. A note on the kitchen table said,

Something came up. I should be back by eight. There's still that bit of trout in the icebox.

This was as close to an outright rebuke as he'd ever received from his housekeeper. Hadn't he said sorry? Not well enough, apparently, if he was being threatened with the specter of leftover trout.

His office bell rang. It was after hours, but then again, he'd been out the entire day. By now, everyone in Birdswing, Barking, and probably parts of Plymouth knew that Mr. Jeffers had suffered a heart attack and Ben had been at his side. Perhaps someone with a lesser complaint had been watching the curb in front of Fenton House, waiting for Ben's car to return.

Still in his coat and scarf, he opened the office door to find Mrs. Garrigan on his front step. It was the first time he'd seen her without the baby since she'd given birth.

"What's this? Where's little Charles?" he asked, ushering her inside.

"I left him with my neighbor. What I mean to say isn't for children's ears. But first, how is Mr. Jeffers?"

"We'll just have to watch and wait. Miss Ernestine Trewin is taking care of him at present, and he couldn't ask for a better nurse."

"You can count on Ernestine," Mrs. Garrigan agreed. "I'll add Mr. Jeffers to my prayers, and her, too. But what I came to say is this."

She paused, took a breath, and forged on with a steely look in her eyes. "I don't want another baby just now. Felix gets flustered, talking of such things, and I'm not sure he understands what I'll be risking when I'm back in the family way. If I die giving birth, I want it to be after Charles is old enough to get along without me." Her voice cracked.

"I disagree that another pregnancy may kill you. With or without more children, it's reasonable for you to expect a normal life."

"I hope so. But Charles needs me now, especially while Felix is overseas," she said. "I've seen that sign in Dwerryhouse's. The one that says Rendell's. I didn't cotton on to what it was until I overheard a man in the pub say if it weren't for Rendell's, he'd be in the poorhouse and his wife would've stuck her head in the oven. If Rendell's can keep me out of the family way, I want it. If not, I want French letters. But I can't ask Mr. Dwerryhouse. I've known him my whole life. I don't want him to think of me as needing—well. That. Will you help me?"

This is where it got tricky for Ben, although Mrs. Garrigan could have no idea. Any man or married woman could walk into a chemist shop and purchase condoms, known as French letters, or contraceptive pessaries, sold under the brand name Rendell's. But few men and even fewer women did. When a couple wanted advice on family planning, the man tended to have a quiet word with his pharmacist or even his barber. Speaking to his doctor was no good. Although the common types of family planning were legally sold, and even euphemistically advertised, they inhabited a gray area legislators preferred to ignore. Instead, politicians dictated to the medical profession, requiring them to behave as if such items didn't exist, except in cases where pregnancy was certain to imperil the mother's life.

Mrs. Garrigan looked him in the eye. "Please. Can you write me a prescription so I can pass it over the counter? So I won't have to ask?"

"Of course," Ben said, and reached for his pen.

Chapter Six

1

4 February 1940

Sunny and springlike, it was a pretty day for a wedding. Not that Mr. Jeffers or the new Mrs. Ernestine Jeffers could tell from inside the venue, that dark, quiet bedroom in Owl Cottage. Juliet, like the rest of Birdswing, was not invited. Ben had allowed the ceremony only after being promised it would avoid too much noise or excitement. This meant no guests, no music, no toasts, and no cake. Mr. Jeffers was required to remain in bed, though Ben helped him into his Sunday coat and stuck a carnation in the top buttonhole. Ernestine wore yellow chiffon, borrowed from her sister, who served as a witness, and both beamed as Father Cotterill said the words. Ben was meant to be the only other witness, but as one of the village's preeminent citizens and someone who could not resist a happy ending, Juliet turned up "accidentally" just before the ceremony (merely to deliver a pie, of course) and remained to watch the couple become man and wife.

"It really is a happy ending, isn't it?" she asked Ben as they walked down Marrow Street toward the High Street and Fenton House.

"You sound like Ernestine. Mr. Jeffers's prognosis isn't dependent upon finding the correct way to phrase the question. If he survives another five weeks," Ben said, "then the worst crisis is past. I won't be able to guess at the damage his heart has sustained until then."

"So you allowed the marriage now because it might be their only chance?"

Ben seemed to consider that. He was matching her long stride fairly well despite his cane, which probably meant the day's warmth was settling into his joints. Before long, he would be putting it aside again. Juliet didn't care either way—to her mind, the cane was distinguished, and hearkened back to a courtlier age—but she knew young men could be peculiar about such things.

"Yes," Ben said at last. "But also because I thought marrying Ernestine would give Mr. Jeffers his best chance at survival. She's already overseeing the butcher shop in an unofficial capacity, and she's enforcing my orders with an iron hand. He tried to get out of bed yesterday and she sent a neighbor to fetch me. By the time I got there, he was back where he belonged, meekly sipping broth like the world's best patient. It's clear to me that he adores her. I think there's a very real chance his heart may repair itself just so he doesn't let her down."

She liked the sound of that. Only yesterday, the rumor of the impending marriage by special license, as there was no time for the banns to be read, had inspired plenty of birdsong, most of it sweet, some of it not.

In Dwerryhouse's chemist shop, Miss Trewin had let slip to a customer that Ernestine had proposed marriage to Mr. Jeffers, rather than the other way around. Not everyone in Birdswing found such an arrangement appropriate, with a few going so far as to say it was further proof the country was coming under petticoat rule. Once, Juliet would've been deeply displeased and waded into the fray herself, but these days she'd begun to think there was no action one could take, or fail to take, that couldn't be criticized by someone determined to find fault. Ernestine had done what was best for herself and her new husband. Having witnessed the joy on the new couple's faces, Juliet felt certain that was what mattered, not a bit of disapproving chatter.

"Look, it's Mr. Dwerryhouse," Ben said. The little man stood outside his shop, sunlight glinting off the colored glass bottles in the window behind him. As they turned the corner onto the High Street, he waved, motioning for them to come over. "I haven't had the chance to speak with him since the letter debacle, have you?"

"No, and I welcome the opportunity," Juliet said. "One can never let misunderstandings fester in a village this size."

"You don't plan to attack him for calling you a liar, do you?"

"Ben! How dare you accuse me of attacking anyone?"

"You attack people daily. You're attacking me now," he retorted, not quite keeping his straight face, and she realized he was teasing her again. Tossing her head, she chose to address Mr. Dwerryhouse, who stood smiling as he awaited them.

"Ideal day for nuptials, wouldn't you agree?"

"Yes, indeed," Mr. Dwerryhouse said. "I look forward to the day Mr. Jeffers is up and about, so I may shake his hand. In the meantime, I sent a few bottles of Iron Brew to Owl Cottage with a note of congratulations. Since he's forbidden spirits, of course."

Before Juliet could reply, Mr. Dwerryhouse said, "Before either of you says another word, please accept my heartfelt apologies for my behavior on Tuesday. It was inexcusable, and I can only beg you both to forgive me."

Such a sterling *mea culpa* never failed to mortify her. She suddenly felt put on the spot, uncertain if she should grant forgiveness or insist there was nothing to forgive. Fortunately, Ben was better at smoothing over these minor hiccups between friends.

"Think nothing of it," he said breezily. "I see you've put salves and lotions on offer. Can I assume springtime in Cornwall can be hazardous to one's skin?"

"I fear so, if one is an unwary rambler or child with bare arms and legs," Mr. Dwerryhouse agreed. "There's giant hog weed, stinging nettles, and wild parsnips, all of which will cause a rash if one's susceptible. A bit of lotion will do for most sufferers, and I'll send those who need greater care to you, Dr. Bones. Only now that I've finished arranging my offerings in the window, I find myself in need of tea. Would the two of you do me the very great honor of joining me?"

They did. Juliet thought they might return to Mr. Dwerryhouse's consulting room, but instead he took them upstairs into his bedsit above the chemist shop. One of the few homes in Birdswing she'd never set foot in, it turned out to be snug and homey, filled with bits and bobs related to his secondary passion, fishing.

After they'd settled themselves around his coffee table, poured the tea, discussed the weather, and shared a plate of McVitie & Price's digestive biscuits, Mr. Dwerryhouse cleared his throat.

"Well. Now. It falls to me, naturally, to address what Aggie would call the elephant in the room," he said. "She was kind enough to call on me Tuesday, you see, after I closed the shop early—"

"'Aggie?'" Juliet repeated. "I thought you were called Aggie, informally, I mean."

"So I am," Mr. Dwerryhouse agreed. "And so was she, when we were both young. Agatha and Augustus became Aggie and Aggie. We were so thick, it gave rise to the general expectation of matrimony. But we were only dear friends. I believe that Tom, God rest his soul, was the only man she ever loved. As for me...."

"Mr. Dwerryhouse," Ben said when the little man seemed unable to continue. "You don't owe us an explanation. We meant no harm when we brought you the letter, but clearly we dredged up memories you preferred to keep private. It was never our intention to force a confidence."

"I know, Dr. Bones, and thank you," Mr. Dwerryhouse said. "Aggie explained that to me. Do you know, she's the first living soul with whom I've ever discussed the matter? All these years, I've pretended it never happened. And the sad truth is, nothing happened in the first place.

"I did have a shop assistant called Bertie years ago. He was handsome and charming, and cruel, when it came to it, but I was the last person to see that. My affection for him was perhaps greater than it should've been, and certainly never returned. Now, over the gulf of years, I can see he viewed me as a sort of patsy, forever lending him money and excusing his shortcomings instead of giving him the sack. In those days, being so young and naïve, I thought I could earn his regard, and then...." He smiled self-consciously. "Then confess the truth. Now I know Bertie guessed the truth about me almost at once, and relied upon it to keep his position and to secure those loans. It took me a year to say, enough. When I did, he threatened blackmail.

"The fact is," Mr. Dwerryhouse went on, looking from Ben to Juliet, "I didn't write that letter. I never breathed a word of my feelings to Bertie or anyone else. I didn't take his threat of blackmail seriously, because my sins were sins of the heart. Again, I must remind you, I was young and naïve. It didn't occur to me that he would simply lie.

"The things he spread about the village shocked me to my very soul. I thought I might be arrested, or driven away. It was around that time that Aggie stopped speaking to me. I thought she believed the lies, but it was only that she was mortified, and had no idea what to say. If only one of us had had the courage to talk about it!" He shook his head.

"But you've renewed your friendship now, haven't you?" Juliet asked. Surely she could find a silver lining if she looked hard enough.

"Yes, we have, at long last," Mr. Dwerryhouse agreed, brightening. "And that's down to the two of you. But I have one more thing to say."

Rising, he went to the bookshelf and returned with a battered leather scrapbook. "This is from 1910 to 1915," he said, thumbing through its yellowed pages, some of which were beginning to crumble. "The fact is, the moment I saw the letter, I recognized the handwriting. I remember the story about that poor man who died in the car crash, too. I heard it from a man who used to run a curiosity shop in Barking. His name was Bryce Pasquette. There he is," Mr. Dwerryhouse said, pointing at a man in one of the photographs. "In front of his shop beside the old rector and some of the WI. Most of them dead, now, or very feeble, I expect."

Juliet looked at the man in the photograph. He was tall and spare, with a long face and a lantern jaw. A shock of hair hung in his eyes, and his clothes were better suited to a laborer than a businessman. Something about his face made her think of a revolutionary, one of those passionate young men who gave out leaflets about the coming rise of the working class.

"You said 'used to run,'" Ben said. "Did he retire?"

"No," Mr. Dwerryhouse said. "I should add that although I considered him a friend, and certainly a clever conversationalist, he never took me into his deepest confidence, nor did I take him into mine. I knew he was carrying on a passionate love affair with some woman in Birdswing, because he turned up here so often, and at various times. I waited for the day I would glimpse them together, or Bryce would share his happy news. But it never happened. Then, one day, I heard that he'd closed the shop and left Barking without a forwarding address. Now that I've seen the letter, I know why, even if I don't know the name of the woman who broke his heart."

"I'm surprised you didn't tell us about him right away," Juliet said, "if only to divert further discussion about you and Bertie."

"I couldn't, out of loyalty to Bryce, even after all these years," Mr. Dwerryhouse said. "He was a goodhearted man, slow to make friends, hesitant to reveal himself, but remarkably decent. I've told you that when Bertie went about, telling his lies, I was terrified of what might befall me. I had no money left to pay his price, so I went to the only shop owner I dared approach, Bryce. It took every drop of courage I had to ask for a loan. He heard me out, and he said no, but kindly. I went away, and the next morning I heard that Bertie had left Birdswing under cover of darkness. Never to return."

"So rather than lend you the money, he paid Bertie off himself," Juliet said.

"So I believe, though he denied it," Mr. Dwerryhouse replied. "How typical of the goodhearted man, to do such a kindness and refuse to speak of it. For a while, I hoped to repay him, but then he, too, went away and never returned." The little man took in a deep breath, exhaled, and smiled at them both. "Aggie told me that if I would simply repeat the story in its entirety, if I would say the words aloud, a weight would be lifted. And it is."

"That's a relief," Ben said. "I've been berating myself for not burning that letter."

"I'm very glad you didn't," Mr. Dwerryhouse said. "Even if I didn't write it, its reappearance has been a blessing. I'm terribly grateful to you both."

* * *

"It might not be spring, technically," Juliet declared as they walked back to Fenton House. "But it's springtime in my heart. Do you suppose it's possible I've become addicted to the happiness of others?"

"I don't know. But as addictions go, you could do worse," Ben said. "If you'd like to make me happy, you have only to go up to the attic, you know. I have patients booked this afternoon, but I'll find a way to steal up there somehow."

"Very well," Juliet said. "Perhaps I'll reread the letter and come up with a list of suspects for the recipient."

Ben groaned. "Just because Mr. Dwerryhouse has chosen to view the intrusion positively doesn't mean we should go about overturning more apple carts. Mrs. Richwine specifically told me to use my judgment. At this point, my judgment is to destroy the letter and forget it."

"Oh, very well," Juliet said, not at all sure she would allow the lost love letter to be destroyed *or* forgotten. She'd tucked it into her handbag for safekeeping, afraid that if she left it with Ben, it would soon be reduced to ashes. "But I've grown rather attached to it for obvious reasons. Probably because I'm still waiting for any sort of missive from you."

Ben seemed not to hear. As he led her through the garden gate and up the stone path toward Fenton House, she waited for a reply with rising irritation. Her nascent addiction to other people's happiness was swiftly giving way to impatience for more of her own.

"Then again, I suppose I may wait forever," she said. "Perhaps you can't be bothered, or the spirit doesn't move you."

He looked sideways at her. "I think you have this muddled," he said, opening the cottage's front door and allowing her to enter first. "Of the two of us, which one is better suited to write a rambling letter full of hyperbole and words you'd need a thesaurus to decode?"

There were almost too many possible ways she could take offense to that question. As she decided which sort of outrage to profess first, Ben hung his hat on the rack, then went to the stairs and called, "Mrs. Cobblepot?"

"I confess, I find your insensitivity on this matter troubling," Juliet said coolly.

Once again, Ben didn't seem to hear. "Mrs. Cobblepot?"

Unwinding his scarf, he went to the kitchen. Juliet heard the back door open and close, and then he reappeared.

"She's out by the shelter, pinning shirts on the line," he told her, smiling as if she were dancing a jig instead of glaring at him. "We have five minutes. Possibly ten, if Mrs. Parry stops by to pass the time of day."

"So," Juliet said in her most withering tone. "Must I assume from your unwillingness to communicate on the matter that I shall never receive a letter approaching any of the sentiments expressed by Mr. Pasquette?"

"Yes. No. I'm not sure," Ben admitted. "When you get like this, I start to get muddled, too. But I'm not going to write a letter." He cupped her face in his hands. "I'd rather just say it. I love you, Juliet. That's all. I love you."

She'd waited so long for him to say those words that when they finally came, hearing them twice wasn't nearly enough. "Tell me again," she whispered. And he did.

Postscript

It was after two o'clock in the morning when Victoria Linton stole downstairs in her dressing gown. Juliet often read late into the night, occasionally roaming about Belsham Manor in search of a new book, a midnight snack, or both, so Victoria had waited until she could wait no more.

Her daughter had come back from Fenton House talking of nothing but Ben, a conversation they'd been obliged to have in secret, given the requirements of her faux marriage. Over dinner, the topic had shifted to Mr. and Mrs. Jeffers, and in the parlor, the after-dinner discussion had been a superficial explanation of Mr. Dwerryhouse's renewed friendship with Mrs. Cobblepot, with no reference to the story about Bertie, which Victoria already knew. It seemed that Juliet had accepted the notion of hole-and-corner, in the Birdswing sense, and fully understood that the matter was never to be spoken of, except under the most dire circumstances. That had given Victoria a little glow of pleasure. Gossip could be irresistible, but she was glad her daughter understood the value of benevolent amnesia, too.

Only after they were in their night clothes and saying good night did Juliet seem to remember one last bit of news.

"By the way," she'd said. "Mr. Dwerryhouse told us who wrote the letter. It was someone called Bryce Pasquette. Apparently, he left Barking years ago and never came back."

It didn't take long for Victoria to find the letter inside her daughter's purse. But it did take her several minutes to gather the courage to open the envelope and withdraw the pages. The moment she saw that handwriting, so familiar even after twenty-seven years, tears sprang to her eyes. Soon they blurred her vision, mercifully obscuring some of the words, but she wiped them away and forced herself to read it all.

"Oh, Bryce," she whispered. "Forgive me."

THE END

From the Author

I hope you enjoyed these novellas about Dr. Bones and Lady Juliet. Their stories will continue in book #4, ***Bones Buried Deep***.

Because I write slowly, readers understandably often ask if I plan on continuing the series. I'm pleased to tell you the answer is an enthusiastic yes. Relaunching the *Dr. Bones Mystery Series* has been a labor of love, and I look forward to writing many more Bones adventures in the years to come. Thank you so much for coming along.

If you enjoyed this book, please consider writing a short review. Honest reviews are literally priceless, and mean the world to a book—and to readers searching for their next read.

Cheers! ·

Emma Jameson

2022

Acknowledgments

The author would like to thank many people for their assistance and encouragement. The list includes, but is certainly not limited to: Cyn Mackley, J. David Peterson, C.D. Reiss, Red Tash, Barbara Franklin, Melissa Meyers, Mary Ellen Wofford, Jenx Byron, and my four cats: Howard, Zahara, James, and Bobby.

Also by Emma Jameson